misfits inc.

no. 1

the vanishing chip

mark delaney

PEACHTREE

ATLANTA

To Robert Larkin
1906-1998
My Grandfather

For your laugh,
For the way you sang an Irish ballad—your voice never wavering,
not even on the high notes,
For the way you took my face in your hands and kissed my forehead,
This is for you.

A FREESTONE PUBLICATION

Published by
PEACHTREE PUBLISHERS LTD.
494 Armour Circle NE
Atlanta, Georgia 30324

www.peachtree-online.com

Text © 1998 by Mark Delaney
Cover photograph of chess pieces and puzzle © 1998 by Ian Christie via The
Stock Market, New York, NY

Book and cover design by Loraine M. Balcsik
Composition by Melanie M. McMahon

Manufactured in the United States of America

10 9 8 7 6 5 4 3 2 1
First Edition

Library of Congress Cataloging-in-Publication Data

Delaney, Mark.
   The vanishing chip / Mark Delaney.
      p. cm.—(Misfits ; # 1)
   Summary: When Mattie's grandfather becomes a suspect in the theft of
   a valuable computer chip, Peter, Byte, Jake, and Mattie, four high school
   students who consider themselves misfits, pool their talents to try to
   discover who really stole the chip and how.
      ISBN 1-56145-176-2
      [1. Friendship—Fiction. 2. Mystery and detective stories.]
   I. Title. II. Series: Delaney, Mark. Misfits ; # 1
   PZ7.D373185Van 1998
   [Fic]—dc21   98-7209
                                                       CIP
                                                       AC

table of contents

Friday, lunch

"get him, Joseph!"
    "Yeah, Joseph, wipe 'im out!"
    Peter Braddock ignored the cheering. He was losing his war against Joseph Vargas. But he would not go down without a fight. He stared at the chessboard in front of him, his hand hovering over one of the pieces.
    Time, he decided, *for some fancy play* off *the board.*
    He quickly made a move—one that hurt his position more than it helped him—and then leaned back in his chair and began to smile. Joseph looked up at him quizzically, and Peter kept on smiling as though his move were the most brilliant chess move anyone had ever played.
    It was the last week of classes, the week before final exams, and the last day of the Ninth Annual Bugle Point High School Lunchtime Chess Tournament. Mr. Blair, the physics teacher, had started the tournament, and it soon became a tradition. At the end of each school year,

the top dozen chess players met in the science lab during lunch, set up the plastic chess sets, and battled for the title of Chess Champion. Usually only seniors played. This year, for the first time, a sophomore had qualified and was competing for the title of champion. That sophomore was Peter Braddock.

Peter watched Joseph study the position of the pieces on the board, searching for a trap. Joseph looked closely at the board, then back at his opponent.

"Your move," Peter said, and then examined his fingernails as though they were far more interesting than Joseph's chess play. Sweat began to form on Joseph's forehead. He reached for a piece, changed his mind, reached for another, then finally made a bad move with his queen. *Good*, Peter thought. *He's still winning, but he's starting to doubt. He thinks I'm up to something.* Peter *was* up to something, but it had nothing to do with where he placed his pieces.

In a little over three minutes the flag on Peter's chess clock would drop, and he would forfeit the game because of time. *Confidence*, he told himself. He picked up a piece and banged it down elsewhere on the board, appearing, he hoped, to know what he was doing. He acted like a player who was winning, although his pieces were very badly positioned. Joseph studied the board for a long time, hesitated, then made another poor move.

The moment Joseph set down his piece, Peter's hand was already moving. He picked up a knight, swept it in an L pattern across two rows of squares, and slammed it right down in the middle of Joseph's territory. *Bam!* Joseph swallowed hard then moved again, and almost before he set down his piece, Peter was charging. He swept in his bishop diagonally—*Bam!*—and Joseph lost a rook. *Bam!* and one of Joseph's knights disappeared. *Bam!* and Peter's pawn was driving away his queen. *Bam!* and the defenses around Joseph's king crumbled.

BAM!

"Check," said Peter.

Silence. No one was cheering for Joseph anymore, and certainly no one was cheering for Peter. Most of the seniors had lost to Peter in the early rounds, and they were, quite frankly, hoping to see the tall, skinny sophomore with the round glasses and the clump of dark hair falling into his eyes lose in the final. Who did this kid think he was, anyway?

Peter knew that Joseph only had two legal moves. If Joseph moved his king one space to the right, Peter would bring down his queen for checkmate. If he moved it one space to the left, Peter would bring down his rook with the same result. Finally, his cheeks burning with frustration, Joseph gave Peter the sign of defeat: He touched his forefinger to his defenseless king and toppled it over. It made a meek tap when it struck the board. Joseph shook Peter's hand, then left the table without saying a word. In fact, all the seniors got up to leave. They crowded around Joseph,

4 clapping him on the back and congratulating him on his play.

None of the students said a word to Peter. He told himself he didn't mind. Once, when he was in the fifth grade, Peter won a countywide spelling bee. The second-place winner was a popular eighth grader from the local middle school. When the contest was over, Peter, his mother, and his father returned to the parking lot to find that someone had soaped the word "smack," a code word often used at Peter's school, across the windshield of their car. A smack was more than just a smart person; it was someone who was *too* smart—smarter than every-one. Smart enough to be disliked.

"Well," said Mr. Blair, "you played an excellent tourna-ment, Peter. Undefeated in five rounds. Congratulations. The trophy is yours." He handed the trophy to Peter, and Peter looked at the bold lettering engraved on the brass plate: Chess Champion. He smiled and tucked the trophy under his arm.

"Thank you, Mr. B."

"Hey, hey, Peter!" a voice called. Mattie Ramiro had been watching the tournament from the back of the lab, quietly passing time by taking apart his Walkman radio and putting it back together. At the start of the game he had eyed a microscope, but Mr. Blair had asked him to leave it in one piece, thank you. Now he rushed to meet Peter, sidestepping the scattered chairs like a cat gracefully strolling through knickknacks on a shelf.

Mattie was a freshman. He stood only about four feet, ten inches tall, and the top of his head barely came to Peter's chest. On Mattie's first day at Bugle Point High, Peter had taken the time to show him where his home-room class was, and somehow Mattie had managed to locate Peter in the break between each class that day. Peter had become Mattie's high school tour guide, although Peter suspected that Mattie was finding his way around just fine. He kept locating Peter, didn't he?

It was not quite true to say that Mattie had become Peter's close friend. He followed Peter constantly. He talked constantly. He needed constant help and attention from Peter. He was sort of like Peter's…puppy dog.

"Peter," said Mattie now, "you were *losing*. I'm no expert, but for a while it looked like Joseph was walking all over you."

The two left the science lab and began making their way to their fifth-period classes.

"Really?" Peter asked. "You thought I was going to lose?"

"You were behind. I *saw*," said Mattie. "You were down a piece, and Joseph had the better position. How did you win?"

Peter frowned as he considered the question. "Sometimes," he said, "I guess it doesn't matter what your position is or how good your opponent is. Joseph *thought* my position was better. He *believed* I was the better player. Once he had that mind-set, he didn't stand a chance."

6   Just then the bell rang. Peter reached into his pocket and removed two folded sheets of paper. He handed them to Mattie.

"These notes are for the others; they're about today. Do you mind?…"

Mattie took the notes and slipped them under the cover of a book. "You got it," he said.

Peter knew the notes would get delivered. Mattie, if nothing else, had proven that he had an occasionally annoying talent for locating people during the five minutes between classes.

They turned to head off to their classrooms, but Peter stopped and watched Mattie as he walked away. "Hey, Mattie," he called, "thanks for hanging around the tournament."

Mattie turned, grinned, and gave Peter a thumbs-up.

As soon as he was out of Peter's sight, Mattie took the notes from his book and stared at them. They made his fingertips tingle. One for Byte. One for Jake. Peter obviously had not written a note for Mattie because Mattie already knew what the notes said. On other occasions Peter told Mattie the news and Mattie delivered notes to the others.

But somehow, Mattie realized, the notes with the weird, scrawled emblem Peter had placed upon them were a sign of membership and belonging. And Mattie didn't get a note, ever.

Mattie didn't feel that the others did not accept him. And yet, the fact that there was no slip of paper with his name on it, no special emblem for him, bothered him immensely at the moment.

No, it wasn't Peter's fault. It was something else. It was the same feeling Mattie had carried with him since he was five years old.

But he wasn't in the mood to think about that.

Friday, fifth period

Although they'd been in class with her all year, hardly anyone spoke to the girl who sat in the very back of the class.

She had long, stringy blond hair and rarely spoke. She often wore high-top sneakers with her dresses. Sometimes her thick-lensed granny glasses with gold wire frames slipped a bit, and she crinkled her nose in an odd way to shift them back up.

And she never went anywhere without her notebook computer.

Today, as usual, she entered from the door in the back of the room. Walking past a long row of her classmates made her stomach tighten—she didn't know what to say to them. They seemed so different from her, chatting and gossiping loudly. The back door was just easier.

She sat down just as the bell rang.

8   Mrs. Mellon walked over to the lectern where she kept her computerized attendance sheets. Every day she bubbled in the names of the students who were absent.

"Jason?"

A football player threw up a hand. "Yeah, here."

"Monica?"

A tiny brunette slid into her seat. "Right here."

Mrs. Mellon continued. She always called out the name of each student and expected each student to respond. The girl with the stringy blond hair had prayed fervently all year that Mrs. Mellon would change that habit. But here it was the last day of school before finals, and Mrs. Mellon was still calling out names.

"Eugenia?"

The girl crinkled up her nose beneath her glasses and drew in a breath.

"Eugenia? Byte?"

She answered almost in a whisper. "Here."

As Mrs. Mellon finished taking roll, Byte opened up her computer, clicked on the database file called "School," and selected "Eng./Per. 5." Mrs. Mellon would be going over the study guide for the final exam, and Byte wanted to be ready. Most of the other students scribbled their notes into spiral notebooks. Byte, however, always typed her notes. She could type faster than she could write, and the computer helped her stay organized.

"The study guide for your final," said Mrs. Mellon, "is on the side chalkboard. You may take the next five minutes to copy it down before we review it."

Byte was almost finished inputting the material. Mrs. Mellon had arranged the class into groups, but Byte usually preferred to work by herself. She began reviewing some of the major literature terms she had learned during the year and stored in her database: *internal conflict, allegory,* and the funny sounding one, *onomatopoeia,* which Byte always remembered by saying "gee-it's-good-ta-see-ya." Each time Byte highlighted a term and selected an icon, her computer program searched out its definition and one or two examples of its use.

Mrs. Mellon walked between the rows of desks and casually glanced at the work the students were doing.

Mrs. Mellon arrived at Byte's desk and looked at her computer. "This plastic casing looks different—darker than before. Have you upgraded from your Toshiba?" she asked.

Byte nodded and continued tapping the keys. At the beginning of the school year, Mrs. Mellon had been a computer novice, but during fifth period she had often paused by Byte's desk to ask a quick question about some glitch she was experiencing on her computer at home. Byte had noticed recently that Mrs. Mellon's problems with the computer were growing less frequent and her questions more sophisticated.

"Yes," said Byte. "My mom's company buys a lot of machines for research, testing for bugs and such." She looked at the teacher and smiled. "Luckily Mom lets me play with the leftovers."

Mrs. Mellon nodded. "Did you have any problems transferring your files?"

Byte shook her head. "Uh-uh. The new version converts them for me. I don't lose any formatting at all."

Byte clicked on a document icon and the hard drive whirred. At the top of the screen, in bold letters, the word *theme* appeared. Below it was a definition, and below the definition were the titles of three short stories the class had read back in September when they were learning about theme. She moved the mouse and clicked again. Now the title of one of those three short stories appeared, followed by the study questions Mrs. Mellon had assigned, the answers to those questions, and the vocabulary words—with their definitions—from the story.

"This is not a standard database," said Mrs. Mellon.

Byte nodded. "Right. The computer came with a database loaded, but it wouldn't let me do some of the things I wanted. I had to modify it a little."

Mrs. Mellon smiled in appreciation. She scooted an empty chair next to Byte, sat down, and looked directly into Byte's eyes. "You know, you have a very special gift, Byte," she said. "Not everyone is blessed with so much talent. You keep using yours, all right?"

Byte's cheeks warmed with the compliment.

Later, when the class period ended, Byte closed her computer, slipped it into its padded carrying bag, and slung it over her shoulder. She grabbed her books and headed out the back door, eyes cast downward as she walked.

As she made her way through the crowded hallway, she felt a finger tapping her left shoulder. She turned, but all she saw were the tired faces of the students filing past her. None of them appeared to want her attention or even looked at her. Byte frowned. She was certain she had felt *something*. Shrugging her shoulders, Byte adjusted the load of books in her arms and continued down the hallway.

As she neared the end of the corridor, she felt the tapping again, this time on her right shoulder. Instead of turning toward her right, she spun impulsively to her left, expecting to catch a certain sneaky freshman in the midst of his getaway.

"Mattie?…" she called.

She saw nothing, just the same faces as before. This time, however, one or two of them seemed a little annoyed that she was slowing down the traffic.

Byte started walking again. She looked momentarily at the computer bag dangling from her shoulder. *That's weird,* she thought. *I would never have left it partially unzipped like that.* A folded paper rested in the snug opening. Mattie had done it again.

She tugged the note from her bag and studied the familiar emblem: a drawing of a square that was both slightly inside and slightly outside a circle. This design was Peter's idea. It was supposed to represent two things that could never fit together, a square peg and a round hole. Below the emblem two words were scrawled: *We're on!*

Byte slid the note into her pocket and smiled.

12

Mattie watched Byte from a distance to make sure she found the message. When she did, he went to his sixth-period class with a smile on his face. He knew that for the next hour, Byte, instead of concentrating on French, would be trying to figure out how he had slipped the note into her bag and how he had gotten away so quickly. *Let her wonder,* he thought. Somehow, the weirder the others thought he was, the more at home he felt with them.

He was in a better mood already.

Friday, sixth period

"Armstrong!" shouted coach Grimes. "Go in for Dennis."

Jake hesitated. *Armstrong. Wow. The coach wants me. He's giving me one more chance.* Jake grabbed his helmet—one of the few that had no scratches or grass stains on it—and tugged it on. *I won't blow it this time.*

Jake lined up at middle linebacker. It did not matter to him that today's game was only a practice scrimmage, or that those were really his teammates on the other side. He had to prove himself. He was bigger, stronger, and faster than nearly all the other players. He knew he was. The coach knew he was. Now he only had to show he was *better.* Today's spring game, part of the tryouts for next year's team, was his last chance to prove it.

The offensive team broke from its huddle, and the quarterback began calling his signals. Jake lined up over the center, Mike Gilbert, a junior who was crouched and ready to hike the ball. The center glared at Jake. Jake knew what he was thinking: *It's only Armstrong. Armstrong the pushover.*

Not this time, thought Jake. *Ignore him. He's trying to psych you out.*

"Two, sixty-eight. Two, sixty-eight. *Hut! Hut! Hut!*"

The center snapped the football into the quarterback's hands. Helmets crashed together as a rush of bodies collided.

Jake watched closely and saw the quarterback run back, twist to his left, and hold out the ball. The halfback ran right into it and gathered it into his gut. The handoff could not have been more perfect.

But Jake—quicker than Mike, better balanced, yet at least forty pounds heavier—faked a move to the right, ran left, and watched the center throw a block at empty air. Jake passed him so swiftly that Mike fell face first into a wet patch of mud where a sprinkler head had leaked. Jake met the halfback at least five yards behind the line of scrimmage. *Hit 'im!* Inside him, his father's voice grew insistent. *Hit 'im cleanly! Make the runner respect you.*

Jake lunged and wrapped his arms around the halfback's knees. All he had to do was drive through with his shoulders, ram them *hard* into the halfback's midsection, and Jake would pancake the guy.

14   But instead of driving the quarterback into the grass, Jake found himself lifting the boy up with one arm and dropping him gently out of bounds. All the practice, all the ability, all the pep talks—none of them meant anything when they ran up against Jake's basic nature.

Mike, who was still lying in the wet grass, looked across the field and shook his head. From fifteen yards away, Jake could hear what he was saying: "What a wimp. Armstrong stinks."

The whistle sounded.

"Armstrong and Gilbert. Get over here. *Hustle.*"

Jake ran to the sideline and yanked off his chin strap. His football uniform, he noticed, was perfectly clean. His helmet still had no scratches on it. He glanced down at the number blazoned across his jersey. It was the number his father had once worn. Jake had specifically requested it. He wondered if maybe he had made a mistake, given himself too much pressure, too much to live up to.

Mike also ran across the field, stopped at the sideline, and removed his helmet. Coach Grimes frowned at Mike. "Gilbert," he said, "You badmouthed other players all last season. You know players on my team *always* show other people respect. That's it—hit the locker room, then turn in your gear."

All the players on the field were silent, their eyes set on Mike. The center, his own eyes wide, said nothing. He turned his red, dirty face to scowl at Jake. His look said *This is your fault.* He tossed his helmet to the ground and walked off the field, picking up his empty gear bag from the bench.

"Jake?"

"Hmm?" Jake had barely heard the coach speaking to him. "What? Oh, sorry coach."

Coach Grimes took a deep breath and looked at Jake as though just now realizing something. "Jake," he said, "take some time out. Have a seat on the bench. We'll talk later."

Jake understood. He had failed to make the team. Oh, he knew what the coach would say: *Maybe a second string offensive position. Or maybe another sport like soccer or cross country....*

Jake squeezed his eyes shut. He had always been muscular and athletic, and these days he regularly ran or lifted weights. Yet he knew the pain and disappointment of losing, and something within him simply refused to be the cause of that feeling in someone else. Jake was uncomfortable in the role of a competitor.

He sighed. At least he still had his music. At a time like this, when thoughts of his father hung over his head, nothing lifted his spirits like playing his clarinet. That idea brought a weak smile to Jake's lips. He figured he'd be playing the clarinet a *lot* when he got home today.

He sat on the bench, and something drew his attention to his gear bag, which was lying at his feet, the name tag staring up at him. He was certain he had zipped it, certain he had left no schoolwork in it, and yet there it was, half open.

16   A folded paper rested inside.

It had to have been Mattie. No one else could have approached the bench by the field, opened his gear bag, placed a note inside, and vanished without anyone knowing he had been there.

Jake opened the note and saw the circle and square emblem at the top and the two-word message underneath. He smiled. It hurt to have failed, to have lost his chance to play on the team next fall, but the message from Peter helped him forget about the hurt—at least a little bit.

Peter, Byte, Jake, and Mattie, he thought. *Square pegs in round holes. Misfits.*

At least they had each other.

they met in the parking lot after school.

Peter leaned against his car while Mattie practiced a card trick on Byte. She watched in amazement as the card she'd chosen appeared in Peter's backpack. Jake walked toward them from the football field. As he walked, he removed a small rubber Superball from his pocket and began bouncing it on the concrete.

Jake usually bounces that ball when something is bothering him. This is a bad sign, Peter thought. *And he's not supposed to be here yet.* The athlete's short blond hair was wet and freshly combed. *Uh-oh. He must have gone to the showers early.*

Jake walked up to them, and Peter decided to say nothing. When the time was right, Jake would tell his friends about the football tryouts.

"Let's roll," said Peter.

"I get shotgun," said Jake, although he always sat in front anyway. He was too large to squeeze into the back seat.

18   Peter's car was a cherry red 1969 Volkswagen Beetle convertible. His father had owned it as a teenager, kept it in dry storage long after its engine had died, and restored it a few months ago when Peter reached driving age. Now it gleamed. Oh, it rattled and creaked in a couple of places, but the upholstery was clean, the paint job was new, and it ran like—well, like a Volkswagen is *supposed* to run. Peter pulled open the passenger door and flipped the seat forward. Byte climbed in. Mattie—the most eager of the group, because today's journey was at his invitation—joined her. Jake snapped the seat back in place and climbed in.

Peter slipped behind the wheel and reached for the sunglasses that hung from the rearview mirror. He flipped them open and slowly slid them on. "Ready?" he asked.

After the shiny new seatbelts were locked into place, the Beetle sputtered to life.

"Friday, and the last day of classes is over," sighed Byte. "This is going to be great!"

The Museum of Modern Science was a glass castle, a magical place as far as Peter, Byte, Jake, and Mattie were concerned. Inside they found a Plexiglas globe that hummed and crackled with blue lightning. Byte touched the globe, and the glowing currents inside tracked the motion of her fingers along the surface. The group passed displays of rocks from the moon and close-up photographs of comet Shoemaker-Levy 9 striking Jupiter. Peter stopped and gazed at the atomic structure of iron on an electron microscope's video screen. Jake walked over to a large metal tube and noticed a brilliant red light shining from the tube in a pencil-thin stream. He placed his hand in the stream, held it there, and a tiny red dot hovered against his palm.

"I'd love to take that thing apart and look inside it," said Mattie, joining him, with Byte and Peter close behind. "That's a laser."

"Yes," said a voice from behind them. "Light Amplification by Stimulated Emission of Radiation. It's quite safe to leave your hand in the beam, of course, because it's only a class two laser. Just heed the warning on the sign and don't look down the barrel. It could cause serious damage to your eyes."

The four teenagers turned toward the voice, but only Mattie recognized it. "Grandpa!" Mattie gave the man a hug. Then he turned to his friends. "Guys," he said, "I want you to meet my grandfather, Vincent Ramiro. He's the one who got us the free admission."

As Mattie started the introductions, Peter began the detective game he often played with his father, who was a special agent for the FBI. *What*, he asked himself, *can I deduce about this man in front of me?* Easy stuff first: Mattie's grandfather was wearing a uniform and badge, and security tools rested in pouches at his belt— flashlight, billy club, walkie-talkie, and a small canister of pepper spray. He was obviously the security guard here at the museum. From his seasoned face and the gray at his temples, Peter guessed the man to be in his early sixties. Now the harder stuff: Mattie's grandfather was fairly tall and well-built. He had a commanding voice. *He may have been a police officer or career military man at one time—ah, yes, that clinches it.* Mr. Ramiro was wearing a gold ring with a Marine Corps insignia on it—*probably a retirement gift.*

"—And this, Grandpa," Mattie was saying, "is my best friend, Peter. He's the smartest guy in the whole school. Peter, this is Mr. Ramiro, my grandfather."

Peter, his face reddening, shook Mr. Ramiro's hand. "My pleasure, sir," he said. "Always an honor to meet a former Marine Corps officer."

Mr. Ramiro laughed. "Officer? I *worked* for a living, son. Master sergeant. Save the 'sir' for someone who's wearing lieutenant's bars." He clapped Peter on the back and ushered the group into the main exhibit area of the museum. "Let me show you around," he said.

Jake leaned in toward Peter's ear and whispered. "Hey, how did you know the old guy used to be a Marine?" Peter just smiled.

Mr. Ramiro led them past a group of visitors to a marble pedestal that rose from the floor in the center of the room. At the top of the pedestal was a display base shaped like a shallow, upside down bowl. On top of that was a tiny object; no larger than a quarter, it was square shaped, and tiny bits of wiring formed a mazelike pattern on its surface. A transparent Plexiglas cube covered the entire display and protected it from dust. Rope barricades kept visitors from getting too close, and Peter could see, if he squinted just right, the crisscrossing red lines of a laser alarm system.

So this was the object they had really come to see. They had heard about it on the evening news. They had read about it in *Omni* magazine. Mr. Blair at school had even spoken about it.

"Wow," said Byte.

"The InterTel 1286dx computer chip," said Mr. Ramiro. "On loan from InterTel Microchips International, the leading computer chip manufacturer in the world."

"I've heard," said Byte, "that it's many times faster than other computer chips."

Mr. Ramiro nodded. "A thousand times faster," he said. "The 1286dx, according to InterTel, will allow computers to do things you can't even imagine." Mr. Ramiro then lowered his voice. Apparently he did not mind sharing the next bit of information with Mattie and his friends, but he did not want to be heard by the crowd that was gathering around. "We're lucky to have it. InterTel has been facing some stiff competition from a couple of other microchip manufacturers. It's lost market share, and its stock is dropping. Our curator was able to cut a deal. InterTel let us display a prototype of the chip. In exchange, they get written up in the newspapers and interviewed on the evening news. The whole world gets to hear about their new chip and how wonderful they are for supporting the museum. It's free advertising—worth a fortune."

"Is this is the only 1286dx they made?" asked Jake.

Mattie's grandfather waved the question away. "Of course not. We still have to have the security, though. If another manufacturer got ahold of this prototype, they might be able to put a 1286 on the market before InterTel can. Or they might improve it, make this one obsolete."

Peter began to slowly walk around the display to see the chip from all sides. He walked around one corner, then another, but when he got to the third side of the cube, the chip *flickered*. It seemed to dance, as though Peter were looking at it through swirling smoke. He blinked. The chip was perfectly fine now. *That was strange.* Peter knew he hadn't imagined that odd flickering. Perhaps it was just a smudge on the Plexiglas, or perhaps the light had been playing tricks on him. Surely—

Then Peter gasped. He heard other people around him gasping as well, so he knew there was no trick of light now.

The 1286dx, in front of at least a dozen witnesses, disappeared from sight. No one had touched it. No one had even gone near it.

It just *vanished*.

Lieutenant Marvin Decker, a detective for the Bugle Point Police Department, had the worst headache of his career. He took a bottle of aspirin from his pocket, swallowed two tablets without water, and grimaced at the bitter taste. "Okay, Sam," he said to his partner, "send in the last one."

They were in the security office of the museum. When the chip had disappeared, Mr. Ramiro promptly locked the doors to keep anyone from leaving, then called the police. Lieutenant Decker and his partner had taken statements from each of the witnesses for the last hour, which was why the lieutenant's head was now aching so badly.

The door opened, and Peter stepped into the room.

"All right, kid," said the detective, "sit down. Make yourself comfortable. This will only take a few minutes…."

The detective asked questions, and Peter told the whole story in as much detail as he could remember. When Peter finished, Sam opened the door and started to escort him from the room.

"Wait," said Peter. He turned and looked at the detective. "Do you have any ideas about what happened?"

Decker shrugged. "We'll take care of it. Go home, kid." He handed Peter a business card that bore his phone number at the police station. "If you remember anything else that might help, give me a call."

When Peter left the room, Decker turned to his partner. "All right," he said, "let's go over what we have."

Sam flipped through the pages of notes he had made. "To begin with, the director stepped out for the afternoon to take his kid to the doctor. I'm stopping by his house later on."

Decker nodded. "Good. Now, all the witnesses gave us pretty much the same story, right? The chip was suddenly gone."

"Right. I figure it's a case of industrial espionage," Sam said. "Somebody didn't like the fact that InterTel was going to revolutionize the industry with this chip, so they decided to do their own research—sticky-finger style."

"Maybe," said Decker. He shrugged. "Refresh my mind about the alarm system."

"Real high-tech stuff. A series of lasers is built into the display box that held the chip. You can't even get close to the display without setting off the alarm. Mess with the lasers, and a computer snaps on."

"What does the computer do?"

Sam smirked. "It calls *us*."

"*What?*"

"Yeah," said Sam. "Sets off the alarm board at the police station. I'm telling you, Marv, this is one serious security system. If anybody gets near that display case or tries to pull the plug on the laser system, we know about it in less than ten seconds."

Decker muttered and shook his head. "That's weird. We didn't get a silent alarm on this one. Someone actually called the precinct to tell us the chip was gone. Isn't that right?"

Sam checked his notes. "Yup. The caller was a Mr. Ramiro, first name Myron, retired Marine."

Decker nodded. "The security guard."

"Yup."

"Interesting. You said the laser system was set to go off if anyone played around with it. Cut the wires, the alarm is set off. Hit the system with a sledgehammer, the alarm is set off. Am I right?"

"Yeah, so?"

"So what happens if you just *turn* the alarm off—with the punch code?"

"In that case," said Sam, "I guess the system would shut itself down, but it wouldn't interpret the shutdown as a robbery attempt."

"The computer wouldn't call us."

"Nope."

Decker began pacing the room. "And who has the punch code?"

Both men stopped and looked at each other. They spoke at the same time.

"*The security guard!*"

"So the prime suspect, then, is this Ramiro guy, the security guard. A retired Marine, for Pete's sake." Decker scowled. "But why would he be involved? It doesn't make any sense." Frustrated, he rubbed his eyes. His head still ached. "You know, Sam," he said, "this one's a real mystery. I hate mysteries. They make my eyes hurt."

Sam nodded. "It's a real mess," he said.

"Where's Ramiro now?" Decker asked.

"He's just outside."

"And you called InterTel?"

"Yeah. I talked to a vice-president," Sam answered. "Guy's name is Finnerman. He's on his way."

"Right," said Decker. He picked up all the written statements they had taken and placed them into a briefcase. Then he looked at Sam and shook his head. "Okay, let's begin investigating our Marine."

Peter could hardly wait to talk to his father.

Nick Braddock came home shortly after Peter returned from the museum. He hung up his coat, walked into his study, locked his gun in a desk drawer, and was a little surprised to find his son waiting for him. Peter was sitting at the antique chess table in the corner, his finger circling the pointed crown on the black queen.

"Hi, Dad."

"Hey, Pete." Nick Braddock sat across from Peter and smiled. Without saying another word, he reached for the pawn in front of his queen and moved it two spaces. Peter moved his own queen's pawn in response. Mr. Braddock leaned back, tapped his forefinger against his lips, then pushed the pawn in front of his queen's bishop.

Peter frowned. "I can take your pawn," he said.

Nick smiled. "You certainly can."

Peter did so, and in a few moves he found he was hopelessly outmaneuvered. "What did I do wrong?" he asked.

Nick reset the pieces into the starting position. "I played a Queen's Gambit," he explained. "I offered you the pawn, and in exchange for it I got a different kind of advantage." He began moving the pieces, both white and black, showing Peter a better method for handling the opening. "Accepting the Queen's Gambit is a tough game, Peter," he said. "It's trouble. You're better off declining it."

Peter nodded silently.

"Now," said Mr. Braddock, "you didn't come into my study just for a chess lesson. What's on your mind?"

Peter told him about the events of the afternoon, describing carefully the disappearance of the 1286dx. Mr. Braddock listened, and his forehead furrowed when Peter told him how the chip had vanished. "Interesting," he said. "That's a pretty high-tech MO for a robbery. Should narrow down the suspects a bit."

"Is there any way the FBI will be handling this case, Dad?"

Mr. Braddock shook his head. "Not likely. Unless the chip is transported over the state line, or the person who stole it commits a federal offense, this theft is not in the FBI's jurisdiction."

Peter understood, but he would have felt better if his father were working on the case.

"You know," Peter said, "maybe I'll just take this case myself. I bet I could figure it out. After all, I've got the highest g.p.a. in my class."

He smiled and hunkered down into an overstuffed easy chair. He closed his eyes, and in his mind he saw a huge chessboard. His opponent, a faceless shadow, reached across the board with a bony hand and moved a

28 piece. *I stole the microchip, Peter,* the figure whispered. *Care to play against me?* Peter touched an imaginary pawn and pushed it forward. As he did, he heard the figure's voice again.

Queen's Gambit, Peter. The pawn is for free.

Mattie was running. He had been sprinting for several minutes. His lungs felt like they were going to explode. His legs felt ready to buckle.

But he refused to stop.

Peter. Got to tell Peter. Peter will know what to do.

Tears streamed down Mattie's face, but he could hardly feel them. He felt the deep ache in his chest and the pounding of his feet on the sidewalk.

Peter....

He turned down a side street. Peter's house was ahead of him, just at the end of the block. A car was in the driveway, and the house lights were on. *Thank God.* He ran up the driveway, onto the porch, and slammed into the front door. He pounded on the door with his fist, and with his other hand he pawed blindly at the doorbell. *Answer!*

Only seconds passed, but they seemed to last forever. The door creaked open, and Mrs. Braddock stood in the entryway, one side of her face yellowed by the light of the porch lamp. Mattie made a choking sound. He slid to the ground and leaned his back against the door frame, his chest heaving.

"Mattie?" Catherine Braddock leaned down to him and touched his shoulder.

The boy gasped a few times, then his head dropped between his knees and he began to sob.

"How many steps is this stinking proof going to *have?*"

Jake looked at the geometry problem in front of him and wished that Euclid had never been born. At least Byte had invited him over to study for finals with her.

The two of them sat at the kitchen table in Byte's home. Byte took a sip of Mello-Yello and flipped through the pages of Jake's geometry book. "Maybe," she said, "you would understand it better if you took the backward approach. Let's look at the answers to the even-numbered problems in the back of the book and see if we can work out how they got them. Then we'll be able to figure out the odd-numbered problems."

"Great," muttered Jake. "It's not like we don't have enough problems to do already. Now we're finding new ones."

But before they could begin working out the geometry problem, the phone rang. Byte checked the Caller ID, then picked up the phone. "Hi, Peter."

Jake could hear the tension in the voice coming from the receiver. Something was wrong. "What?" Byte said. Her voice rose in alarm when she spoke. "When? Now? I suppose so. What hap—" She stopped in midword. Peter must have cut her off. "Okay," she said, "we're on our way. I'll call back if there's a problem." She hung up the phone and looked at Jake. "Can you drive us to Peter's house?"

"No problem."

The two of them scrambled for jackets, and Byte called up the stairs. "Going over to Peter's, Mom." She didn't wait for an answer.

They arrived ten minutes later. Mrs. Braddock let them in, and they raced up the stairs to Peter's bedroom. Mr Braddock stood just inside the open door. Peter was sitting at his desk, and Mattie was collapsed on the floor, his arms wrapped tightly around his knees. His face was so pale that it took on a bluish tint from Peter's fluorescent desk lamp. The younger boy sniffled once and turned to look at Jake and Byte.

"The police arrested my Grandpa," he whispered. "They think he stole the computer chip."

Peter stood and walked to the center of the room. "We all saw what happened at the museum. The chip disappeared. This was not some simple theft. It required extensive planning."

"More than planning," said Mr. Braddock. "Your thief stole a high-tech device, and he seems to have used a high-tech means to accomplish it. There are just not that many people who could have pulled it off—not without inside help."

Mattie looked up. "That's what the police were saying. They said it had to be someone on the inside. They said someone had to have turned off the alarm system."

Peter shook his head. "Nonsense. The alarm system was working when the chip disappeared. I saw it." *So how was the chip stolen? How does a thief get past a laser security system and a Plexiglas display case? How do you make something disappear in front of a dozen witnesses?*

Mr. Braddock gripped the knob on the bedroom door, then turned and looked back at Mattie. "If you need anything, Mattie," he said, "you let us know. I'll tell the police that the FBI will help in any way they can."

Mattie nodded. "Thanks."

Peter shut the door as his father left. When his father's footsteps faded down the stairs, he turned to Mattie. "Mattie," he asked quietly, "where's your grandfather now?"

"At home," said the younger boy. "Grandma took some money out of my college savings and bailed Grandpa out of jail. The trial is in one month." His eyes dropped to the floor.

I bet the thief will disappear before that. We'll have to act quickly, Peter thought. His voice became deadly earnest as he looked at each of his friends. "Someone has stolen the chip and framed Mattie's grandfather. I'm for figuring out who that someone is. Can I count on you to help me?"

Jake's mouth, Peter saw, had tightened into a grim line. "I'm in," he murmured quietly, looking at Mattie.

Byte nodded. "Square pegs in round holes," she said. "Count me in."

Peter sat down again, and he stared through the bedroom window at a warm, starry sky. He wasn't sure what a detective would do next, but he did know that he and his friends had to figure out how the 1286dx had been stolen. Once they figured out the *how,* they had a much better chance of nailing the *who.*

three

Monday morning

the elegant man had wavy silver hair. He wore a designer shirt, a silk tie, and a custom-tailored Italian suit. For the next few minutes, it was necessary to create an impression of vast wealth. It had to be a casual impression—as though he were so wealthy he did not have to *think* about money.

He was, in fact, quite wealthy, but he was *always* thinking about money—having more than anyone else, and enjoying every luxury money afforded him. The first of these obsessions had brought him to Bugle Point, and the second to this house in particular.

"I'm Malcolm Roarke," he said to the real estate agent. "It's a pleasure to make your acquaintance." He had lived all over Europe, so he was able to affect a vaguely foreign accent to impress her. "You must be Mrs. Espinoza."

Mrs. Espinoza nodded and smiled. She made her living selling houses—or renting them, in this case—and the more expensive the house, the more money she made. Malcolm Roarke knew that she was very happy to meet him. The house they were standing in right now was *very* expensive.

The agent offered her hand to him, and Roarke shook it. He smiled and deliberately allowed the smile to be flirtatious. Mrs. Espinoza began to blush. He noticed that she had to catch her breath before she could speak.

"You told me on the phone," she said, waving her hand in front of her warm face, "that you were looking for quite a nice place to rent. A place that was secluded. You also said you wanted an elaborate security system."

"Yes, that's it exactly."

The house they were in was a mansion. It sat on a bluff overlooking Bugle Point, and it was set back off a winding road, hidden behind a grove of mature pine trees. It could not have been more perfect. "I value my privacy," said Roarke. "I also value my antiques and my rare stamp collection. I wish to protect them from…intruders."

Yes, he had many antiques and a remarkable stamp collection. Malcolm Roarke loved *things,* and he had acquired many. Indeed, he loved his possessions so much he could not bear to be away from them. He would bring many of his favorite items here, although he only planned to stay a few weeks.

Roarke dipped his hand into his pocket and fingered a key. The key fit a safety deposit box, and within the box was an object barely larger than a nickel. The object was flat in shape and crisscrossed with micro-thin wiring. Roarke smiled as he pictured it resting in its protective plastic on a bed of velvet cloth. Soon he could bring it here and hide it safely. He rubbed his thumb across the key's flat surface as though it were a lucky rabbit's foot. "Show me the security system," he said, flashing his most charming smile.

Mrs. Espinoza led him to a small room. In it were a dozen television screens. Connected to these screens was a vast system of rotating video cameras. From this room, Roarke could see just about every square foot of the house and grounds.

"Perfect," he said.

"The previous owner was an art collector," said Mrs. Espinoza. "He owned several Picassos. He spared no expense in putting this system together. When he passed away, his daughter decided to rent the house for a while until she was ready to move back in."

Malcolm Roarke nodded. He would live here in luxury for a little while until the heat from the robbery died down. Then he would quietly fly back to Europe, meet with his…business associates, and sell the 1286dx for a cool fifty million dollars.

The real estate agent noticed his hesitation. "The rent *is* quite high," she said, "but—"

Roarke silenced her with a wave of his hand. "Not at all," he said. "I'll take it. When do I sign the lease?"

Yes, his dreams were about to come true.

And he would be an ocean away before anyone figured out how he had pulled it off.

Peter turned in his fourth-period physics exam and rubbed his eyes. He had stayed up late last night, but spent more time thinking about the computer chip than studying for Mr. Blair's final, which had turned out to be a monster. Only a minute or two remained in the period, and Peter returned to the lab table and rested his head on his arms to think until the bell rang.

All right, he told himself. *One more time: What do we know for certain?* The question was painfully easy to answer: *We know the chip is gone, and we know almost nothing about how it was stolen.*

Peter, his eyes closed, again vividly saw in his mind the chip, the thick acrylic cube, and the laser beams that crisscrossed the display. He saw where he and his friends were standing around the exhibit. He saw again the odd flickering that preceded the chip's disappearance, and then he watched as the chip vanished.

So how did it disappear?

Peter had asked himself this question perhaps a hundred times since the theft. He and his father had discussed dozens of possibilities, and his father had provided a lengthy description of how the laser security system worked, but they always ran into a technological dead end. Peter needed to talk to someone else and find a fresh way of looking at the problem. When the bell rang, he waited until the classroom emptied, pacing around the room while Mr. Blair loaded the final exams into a briefcase.

"Something on your mind, Peter?" the teacher asked.

Peter decided to get right to the point. "Mr. Blair," he asked, "did you hear about the disappearance of the 1286dx computer chip?"

Mr. Blair pressed his finger against the nose bridge of his glasses. Peter recognized the gesture; it meant that Mr. Blair had been thinking about this subject for some time. "I saw it on the news last night," he said. "I'm sorry to hear about Mattie's grandfather."

Peter nodded. "Mattie's taking it pretty hard." He was silent for a moment. "Mr. Blair," he blurted out, "how could the chip just vanish like that? I was there. I saw it. No one was anywhere near it. How could it just disappear?"

Mr. Blair smiled. "Back in the 1920s," he said, "Harry Houdini, the famous stage magician, made a live elephant disappear. A few years ago, a magician named David Copperfield made the Statue of Liberty disappear—live, on television."

Peter sat down. "You're saying it was a trick?"

"Peter," said Mr. Blair, scratching at his beard, "any nine-year-old with a library card and the patience to practice can make a coin or a playing card disappear. Does that mean the coin has ceased existing?"

"Of course not," said Peter. "But the nine-year-old is just doing a simple sleight of hand trick, hiding the card someplace out of sight. What happened at the museum was more *complicated*."

Mr. Blair nodded. "Agreed," he said. "But based on the account of the theft I heard on the news, I think the difference is only one of scale. I believe your thief just performed sleight of hand on a grander level. Tell me, Peter—in general, how does a magician cause an object to disappear?"

Peter took a deep breath before replying. "Well, the object is actually there in front of the audience, and the magician, using smoke and mirrors or whatever, makes it appear that the object is gone when it really isn't. It's up his sleeve, or it's in the hand that's supposed to be empty."

"Exactly," said Mr. Blair.

"So you're saying the chip didn't really disappear? That it went up somebody's *sleeve?*"

Mr. Blair shrugged. "That's an oversimplification," he said, "but you're essentially correct. The thief could have used mirrors, though I haven't the slightest idea how he'd make it work. Or there could have been some kind of opening in the display case, allowing the chip to fall out of sight."

"Hmm. I don't think so," said Peter. "I would have seen it drop. Instead, it just vanished."

Mr. Blair thought for a moment. "The problem is that all these magic techniques require a distraction—a bright light or a loud sound—to pull your attention away for an instant while the trick actually works.

According to your description of the event, there was no distraction."

Now that he was working constructively on the problem, Peter's energy started to return. "Wait a minute," he said. "There's another way. The magician can go in the opposite direction. He can make the audience believe the object is there when it really *isn't*."

Mr. Blair nodded, rising from his desk and heading toward a cabinet in the back of the room. "Follow me, Peter," he said. "I may have an idea about that, too."

He rummaged around in the cupboard and removed a plastic object. It was about eight inches in diameter, circular, and looked like a toy flying saucer, or like two bowls—one upside down and placed on top of the other. He set it on his desk, flipped a switch at its base, and gestured for Peter to take a better look at it. Peter did so. On top of the plastic object, bright and shiny as could be, was a quarter.

"What's this?"

Mr. Blair pointed. "Pick up the quarter," he said.

Peter reached for the coin—*and his hand went right through it!*

Peter felt nothing but air. When he moved his hand away the quarter was still on top of the object, but Peter's fingers passed right through it as though it were a ghost.

Mr. Blair chuckled. "It's a virtual image, Peter," he said.

"What does that mean, exactly?"

"A virtual image—a hologram—is a reflection like you'd see in a mirror, only it's three-dimensional. Look."

40

Mr. Blair lifted up the top half of the object, and Peter saw that this bowl-shaped half had a hole in its center about two inches across. Somehow, when the object's two halves were locked together, this hole became quite invisible.

But the object's bottom bowl was more interesting. Its inside was mirrored, and in the center of it lay a quarter—a real one.

"You can buy complex holograms that actually appear to move," said Mr. Blair. "They're sophisticated and require a small laser." He handed the bowl assembly to Peter. "But this hologram is a simpler design. See that hole in the top half? Light comes through that hole, and the curved mirror inside the unit reflects back a three-dimensional image of the quarter." Then he smiled. "You tried to grab a reflection, Peter."

Peter's heart was pounding. "You think the 1286dx that disappeared might have been a hologram?"

"Could be. Solid objects don't just vanish, Peter. The laws of physics won't let them."

"But even if it were a hologram, it would have to reflect the real chip, right? And if the real chip was being reflected, and the alarm didn't go off, how did the chip's hologram—and therefore the real chip also—disappear at that moment?"

"I couldn't tell you. That's why I haven't spoken to the police about any of this. It's all fairly wild speculation."

Peter's mind raced, his thoughts practically tripping over one another, but after a few moments his ideas all crashed at the same dead end. Mattie's grandfather was the only person with the code to the display, and therefore the only one with access to it. But Peter simply refused to believe that Mr. Ramiro was the thief.

Peter put the hologram toy back together. The hole in the plastic became invisible again, and the ghost-quarter magically reappeared on the saucer's top. Grimacing, Peter stabbed his finger right through the center of the false projection.

I'm going to figure this out, he told himself, *if it takes forever.*

But he knew Mr. Ramiro couldn't wait that long. The investigation would have to start that afternoon.

The corridor was crowded with students rushing to finals, but Mattie slipped between them the way soap slips through wet fingers. Most of the students did not notice him. He twisted his body sideways, stepped between two people, and fell in behind a tall senior, the captain of the boys' basketball team. Mattie remained behind him for a while and let him run interference. At least until he found…

"Peter!"

Mattie waved and called Peter's name again; Peter would never be able to see him otherwise. "Hey, Peter, over here."

Peter waved back, and Mattie wriggled through the crowd to reach him. The younger boy remained silent as the two left the corridor and walked outside to the quad.

42 Mattie saw Peter take note of his outfit, and Mattie glanced down at himself. He hadn't bothered to change his clothes from yesterday.

Peter removed some folded slips of paper from his jacket pocket. "Listen," said Peter. "I need you and the others. We'll meet again this afternoon."

Mattie took the notes. He was confused for a moment when he realized there were three slips of paper instead of two.

"Three?" he asked.

Peter looked at him. "You're part of the group, aren't you?"

Mattie stared back at Peter, silent for a moment. Then he looked at the notes. One had his name on it. It also bore the circle and square emblem of the group. *I'm now officially a Misfit.*

"Thanks, Peter," he said quietly. The extra note was a little thing, but it marked the first time Mattie had ever felt like an equal.

"Come on," said Peter, "I'll walk you to your next class."

They walked across the quad without speaking for a few moments. Then Peter broke the silence. "How's your grandfather doing?"

"He's mostly mad," said Mattie. "No one's ever questioned his honesty before." After another long silence, he said, "They put him on leave from his job at the museum until the case is solved. Grandma's half-crazy, she's so upset."

Peter nodded.

"You know," Mattie went on, "my parents got divorced when I was five. Everything was just so upside down, so *insane.* I didn't really understand it all. My mom moved to Rhode Island, and my dad moved to California. They put a whole country between them. I screamed and cried so much.… I guess neither knew how to handle me on top of the divorce, so they let me stay at my grand-parents' house for a little while. But I never moved. My grandpa is my *dad.*" Mattie felt his eyes burn and then start to tear, but he quickly wiped the drops away. He pretended to look at some birds pulling apart a ham-burger bun someone had dropped on the grass at lunch.

"You'll get the notes to Jake and Byte?" asked Peter after a moment.

Mattie gave Peter the thumbs-up. "No problema," he said quietly.

They walked back inside to Mattie's classroom, and Peter turned to go to his own class. Mattie stopped him before he left. "Peter, why is this happening?"

Peter shook his head, and Mattie understood.

Not even Peter knew the answer to that one.

Byte found Peter's note tucked right inside her closed notebook computer as she was leaving her math final. Mattie was playing games with her again. Somehow that squirrelly freshman had managed to get inside her com-puter bag, open the computer, and leave the note folded neatly across the keyboard, all without her seeing him.

44 She read the note and rushed through the hall even faster. So, they would be meeting again. Byte had to notify her mom before she left with the others.

She pushed through the glass doors that led into the school's administration offices. The principal's office was here, and the deans' offices were just down the hall. Byte walked right past them. She was looking for Mrs. Calder, the assistant in the counselor's office.

She was a pushover when Byte needed to use the phone.

Mrs. Calder sat at her desk. Her hair was piled up and teetering high on her head, hair sprayed until she could crack walnuts on it, but Byte did not stare. She was used to it.

"Hi, Mrs. Calder."

The assistant leaned back in her chair and smiled. "Hello, Byte," she said. The expression on her face said that she already knew Byte was about to press her for a favor. "And what can I do for you today?"

Byte tried to look sheepish. "I need to call my mom, please."

"Now, now," said Mrs. Calder, "you know I'm not supposed to do that. There's a pay phone just outside for student use." She always tried to sound firm when she said such things, but Byte knew better. Mrs. Calder was about as firm as a marshmallow, and just as sweet.

"Aw, Mrs. Calder," said Byte, "you know that rule doesn't apply to *me*. My situation is *different*."

Mrs. Calder, smiling, slid the phone across her desk so Byte could reach it more easily.

In a way, Byte was correct. Byte's mom worked during the day as a software engineer for a multimedia company. She was often busy when Byte tried to call, so they had arranged a different way to communicate with each other: Byte, using her notebook computer, sent her mom e-mails.

E-mailing her mom was easy. Byte connected the cord from Mrs. Calder's phone into the modem jack on the back of her computer. Then she opened up the computer, turned it on, accessed her online provider, and in moments was ready to send a message. She typed a quick note explaining where she was going and when she would be home, then sent the message on its way. And best of all, there was no voice at the end of the phone line telling her she couldn't go.

When the computer signaled that the e-mail had been sent, Byte shut it down and disconnected the phone cord. She turned Mrs. Calder's phone around, plugged the cord back into it, and slid it across the desk to her. "Thanks," she said, but one more favor was on her mind. "Um, may I?…" she asked, looking at the candy jar.

Mrs. Calder breathed a deep sigh, smiling and shaking her head. Byte knew she kept the jar of jelly beans on her desk more for the students than for herself. Mrs. Calder reached for it now, set it down in front of Byte, and removed the glass lid.

Byte took the last purple one.

46   Jake sat down for his fifth-period geometry final and flipped through the pages of his binder to cram for a few last moments. He was a little worried about the final; his mind sometimes drifted while his teachers spoke. Sometimes he found himself mentally practicing the clarinet solo he was working on in band or pondering the odd ticking he had heard in his car's engine that morning.

He riffled to the geometry section, and a note slipped out and fell to the floor. The note had to be from Peter. They always were. *But how,* Jake asked himself, *did it get into my notebook?* He shook his head. *Mattie.*

Jake unfolded the note. They were meeting again at Peter's house this afternoon. Good. Jake did not really know Mattie's grandfather, but he had a good feeling about the man. He felt he should help in any way he could.

But first, he told himself, *I have another matter to attend to. After finals today, I'll have to go home and have a little talk with my father, to explain why I probably won't be a member of the Bugle Point High School football team next year.* Jake dreaded the conversation. For as long as he could remember, he had seen his father's football trophy on the mantel over the fireplace in their family's living room. The trophy was tall, showing a quarterback raising his arm to throw. It was made of solid brass that had tarnished over the years, turning a greenish-gold.

And how will my dad feel about my failure? he wondered. He took the pile of tests as it came to him, removed one from the top, and passed the pile to the person behind him. He was already wishing he were someplace else.

His dad was sprawled on the living room sofa when Jake came in through the front door. Mr. Armstrong, a salesman for a large printing company, visited major accounts all over the state and took orders for printed products like business cards, signs, and mailing labels. He was often on the road, but sometimes, when business allowed, he came home early.

Jake had often heard his father telling his mother how difficult the business was, how boring, and how he would like to be his *own* boss and come home *every* evening. But Mr. Armstrong had taken the job straight out of high school. Time passed. Wedding bells rang. House payments gobbled up paychecks. And Jake was born. The job had become a necessity.

"Hi, Dad."

"Hey, Jake."

Jake wasn't sure how he would break the news to his father. He stood there, blank-faced, and then the words just bubbled out of him. "Dad," he said, "I don't think I'm going to make the football team."

His father sat up and rubbed his eyes. "Hmm?"

"They haven't posted the final cut or anything, but—" Jake shrugged his shoulders and shook his head.

His dad paused before speaking. "How's that make you feel?"

That was an unexpected question. "Well—bad, I guess." He wasn't lying. Jake did feel bad, but he realized then that it was not himself he felt bad for. He had not disappointed himself. He really wasn't all that crazy about football; truth be told, he'd rather just stick with jazz band and his clarinet. "I'm okay. I just—well, I just didn't want you to be disappointed in me."

Mr. Armstrong again rubbed his fingers over his eyes. When he finished, his gaze turned toward the coffee table, where he had left his car keys, his tattered appointment calendar, and the little notebook which recorded all his mileage and expenses. "Listen," he said finally, "when it comes to your hobbies, you do what you want to do. Football was an enormous part of my life in high school—it doesn't mean it has to be a part of yours. You gotta make your own decisions about who you want to be." He looked at Jake with a strange intensity. "And don't worry. I won't be disappointed."

Jake nodded, and his father lay back down. Jake noticed, however, that his father did not close his eyes. Mr. Armstrong lay on the couch, his arms stretched behind his head, his eyes open. Jake wondered if he was listening to what his own inner voices were saying.

Jake closed the door to his bedroom and placed a jazz CD in his stereo. With his headphones on, he sat on the floor with his back against the wall and removed the Superball from his pocket. He bounced it so that it struck the floor, ricocheted off the wall, and arced toward the ceiling before landing again in his hand. Jake relaxed in the movement of the ball, the steady rhythm of its bouncing, and the faint vibration when it struck the hardwood floor.

He closed his eyes and thought about Mattie's grandfather and the chip. Later—tonight—he would practice his clarinet.

When the others arrived, Peter already knew exactly what they needed to do. "Byte," he said, "since you have the computer, would you see what you can find out about InterTel, please?"

She pulled her computer from its nylon bag and switched it on, the glowing screen casting a flickering blue light across her face and glasses. Peter could see the words on the screen reflected in tiny, warped letters on her lenses.

Byte, Jake, and Peter had each stumbled through the first quarter of their freshman year, overwhelmed by the newness of high school and never quite fitting in or feeling comfortable with their fellow students. Finally, they had stumbled onto each other and had gradually become friends. And last fall Mattie had joined them.

Peter had always been the leader. But there had never been so much at stake before. Mattie's grandfather was in serious trouble. The self-confidence Peter so carefully cultivated wavered a little.

Byte looked up when she was finished. "There's an InterTel Web site, and I looked at the Dow Jones too," she told him. "Mattie's grandfather was right. InterTel's sales figures took a big dive last quarter, and its stock has lost twenty percent of its value over the last two years. The company is hurting."

"Are they hurting badly enough so that people inside the company might...you know, steal the chip and get what they can before the company goes under?"

"It's possible, I guess," said Byte. "Another microchip designer, Digicomp, has been stealing away a lot of the market. The 1286dx is supposed to be InterTel's salvation."

"I think we should break up into teams," Peter said. "Jake, you and I are going downtown tomorrow. We're going to pay a visit to the offices of InterTel, and we're going to talk to a guy named Bill Finnerman to see what else we can find out about the chip. I called InterTel this afternoon. This Finnerman guy was in charge of the exhibit at the museum." He turned to Byte. "Byte, I want you and Mattie to go to the library and find out everything you can about mirrors, magicians' disappearing acts, and holograms."

Mattie frowned. "Holograms? You mean like on Marvel Universe Trading Cards?"

"Right," said Peter. "Like the three-dimensional chase cards. Also, see what you can find out about other kinds of three-dimensional images—like the Captain Eo movie at Disneyland, stuff like that. It might be important."

Byte gave Peter a quizzical smile. "What's all this about?" she asked.

"Yeah," said Jake. "I don't get it."

Peter drew in a deep breath. He told the others all about Mr. Blair and the theories they'd discussed about the theft, especially about the hologram. He explained his ideas about how the criminals might have committed the robbery. "We can't afford any mistakes. These thieves are clever enough to make the 1286dx disappear. There's no telling what they might do to us."

yte and Mattie stepped off the bus and entered the two-story, red brick building.

"Tullahook County Library, Bugle Point Branch," Byte said, sighing. "I don't think I've been here since I was nine years old."

"Don't you read?" asked Mattie.

Byte punched him lightly in the shoulder. "Of course. I go to the school library, or I buy books so I can keep them."

"I come here all the time," Mattie said, walking purposefully toward the back of the building.

"Tell you what, then," Byte said, her nose crinkling to push up her glasses, "just do your thing, then bring whatever you find back to that table there. I'll join you when I'm finished."

Byte knew the library had made some concessions to the twenty-first century, such as replacing the old card catalog with CD-ROM and installing docking ports for Internet browsers. Let Mattie get ink smudges on his fingers. She'd do a little Net surfing instead. She figured she'd be halfway finished before Mattie located his first magazine. She plugged in her computer, and in no time she had accessed her Internet provider and made her way onto the World Wide Web. Cyberspace, unlike a library, wasn't held together by walls. There was almost no limit to what Byte could find, given enough time and a little curiosity. After exploring the topics of magic, vanishing, mirrors, Captain Eo, and 1950s 3-D horror movies, however, she'd found little that seemed applicable, and soon searched out the topic of holograms. Eventually she found a chat room frequented by physics majors from Cal-Tech and MIT and waited patiently while they shared very technical information.

Then she started asking questions.

One of the college students, who was preparing a thesis on holograms, recommended a definitive article in the *Journal of Physical Science,* which the student said was on-line. Byte slipped from the chat room and keyed in the journal's Web site address. *Bingo.* There in the current issue was an article entitled "Light/Shadow Enhancement in Three-Dimensional Holographic Imaging." Byte didn't know exactly what it meant, but it sure sounded like it might be important. She selected the page number, ordered a download, and watched as the screen flickered and the article appeared.

But something strange was happening. Byte frowned. The text of the article, which was in neat columns moments ago, began swirling like a whirlpool. The letters spun dizzily, dissolving into an eerie red vortex that sucked the article away. Byte gaped. A bestial face, a virtual demon from hell, leaped to the screen. The face had empty sockets for eyes, a huge, gaping mouth, and a thick, pointed tongue. The tongue wavered in the air like a snake.

Byte, shaken, drew back from the terrifying image and began to shut down the computer and go find Mattie. Through the tiny speakers inside her computer, the demon began to laugh.

While Byte and Mattie were at the library, Peter and Jake pulled up to InterTel Microchips International. The building was a ten-story glass monolith. Gardeners had groomed the grass and trimmed the bushes. Pink roses bloomed. On the surface, InterTel was a very beautiful place.

Jake frowned. "Gives me the creeps," he said.

"Yes," Peter said quietly. Perhaps it was the building itself that seemed so foreboding. It was cylindrical in shape and finished in polished black glass. With the elevator shaft jutting from its side, it looked like the barrel of a huge gun pointed at the clouds.

The receptionist looked up from her desk when they entered the building. "May I help you?"

Peter stepped up to the desk and squared his shoulders. For some reason, he thought he should look as tall as he possibly could. "Yes," he said. "Could we please speak to Mr. Bill Finnerman?"

"Do you have an appointment?" she asked, scanning her monitor.

"No," Peter replied, "but—"

"I'm sorry," she interrupted. "Mr. Finnerman is very busy. If you'd like to schedule an appointment with his assistant, you may call her sometime next week," she said curtly.

But Peter had prepared himself for a refusal. He had assumed that it would not be easy to get in to see the man.

"I understand he's busy," he said, smiling, "but this is very important. I'm sure it's a matter of great concern to him."

"Really, I'm sure it is," said the receptionist.

"We witnessed the microchip robbery at the museum. We have information that Mr. Finnerman will find very helpful."

The receptionist sighed and pushed a button on the intercom. "Sheryl?" she said. "This is Liz in the lobby. There are two boys out here asking to see Bill. They say they were at the museum when the chip disappeared."

After a long pause, a man's voice—Mr. Finnerman's, no doubt—came over the intercom. "Send them up."

The receptionist held up a pen. "Sign in here, please."

She handed each boy a visitor's badge. "Elevator's down the hall. Eighth floor. Second office on the left." She turned back to the telephone switchboard next to her appointment monitor.

Peter nodded toward the hallway and winked at Jake. "Let's go," he said. "I guess Mr. Finnerman isn't as busy as she thought."

Amazingly, the executive let the boys into his office almost immediately. Fine art prints decorated the walls. The desk was cut from exotic hardwoods, inlaid with mother-of-pearl.

"Um—have a seat," Mr. Finnerman said. "Make yourselves comfortable."

"Thank you," said Peter. As he and Jake sat in the large seats opposite Mr. Finnerman's desk, Peter scrutinized him. Fat and balding, he wore an expensive white dress shirt a fraction of a size too big for him. It settled like a tent around his waist and the shoulder seams fell perhaps an inch lower than a tailor would have liked. His pants were cut from a fine herringbone fabric and ironed to a sharp crease, but they had wide pleats in the front that ballooned out when Finnerman sat, emphasizing the man's weight problem. Dark red silk, his tie was far too busy for the pants. *Essentially,* Peter concluded, *Bill Finnerman seems to have expensive taste in clothing but lacks the somewhat subtler taste required to really look well-dressed.*

Worse, the man wears too much cologne, Peter noticed. The office reeked of one-hundred-dollar-an-ounce manly musk.

Mr. Finnerman fiddled with some papers on his desk. He arranged them one way, then another, and finally left them in the place where they had been originally. "So, what can I do for you boys?"

"I'm Peter Braddock and this is Jake Armstrong," said Peter. "We're here because we saw the disappearance of the 1286dx. Quite an amazing piece of technology."

"Yes, well," said Mr. Finnerman, smiling. "The advancements our engineers have made in using copper as a conductor rather than silicon have been ground-breaking and helped lead to the development of the 1286dx...." His smile faded. "The theft has hurt us very badly—and it's certainly been an embarrassment for me, since it was my idea to let the museum display the chip in the first place. But that's all a matter for the police now, isn't it? I understand they have a suspect already."

Peter nodded. "That's true," he said, "but the man's innocent. He didn't steal the chip."

Mr. Finnerman looked directly at Peter. For just an instant, his left eyelid fluttered. Peter wasn't even sure he had really noticed it. An instant later Finnerman raised his eyebrows. "That's news to me, son," he said. "I've been in touch with the police about this matter, and I haven't heard anything about another suspect in the case."

The surprise on Mr. Finnerman's face had seemed genuine enough, but what was it that Peter saw *beyond* the surprise? A flash of worry? Peter's attention moved

58 then to the desktop, and particularly to Mr. Finnerman's open briefcase, but nothing seemed unusual. Peter noted file folders, a cell phone, and an electronic organizer. Everything looked normal.

So why was the man sweating so profusely in a cool, air-conditioned office?

"We believe," Peter went on, "that the suspect in the case was framed."

There was that strange tic again, that odd fluttering in Finnerman's eye as he asked, "Do you have any evidence to support this?"

Just then the intercom on his phone buzzed. Mr. Finnerman leaned forward and touched a button. "Excuse me," he said to Peter and Jake. "Yes, Sheryl?"

His assistant's voice came through the speaker. "Mr. Finnerman, the documents you've been waiting for have arrived. Can you sign them right away?"

Finnerman threw a quivering smile at the boys. "Sorry," he said. "You'll have to excuse me for a moment." He rose from his desk and left for the outer office.

Finnerman had barely passed through the door before Peter was out of his seat and around the desk. "Watch the door," he said to Jake. "Give me a warning when he comes back." He began carefully picking through the papers in Finnerman's briefcase.

"Peter!" Jake whispered fiercely. "Are you crazy?" His voice dropped to a thinner whisper as he stepped toward the door. "What if he—"

"Sssh," said Peter. "Just watch for him."

Jake moved nearer the door to keep watch. "What are you looking for?"

Peter continued quickly rifling through the case. "I don't know," he hissed. "The guy's acting very strangely. I want to see if he's hiding something."

Next Peter searched the desk drawers. Nothing. He looked at the computer on Finnerman's desk. He would have loved to click through its files, but there wasn't time. His eyes circled the office.

A two-drawer filing cabinet rested in a corner. Peter tugged hard at one of the drawers, but the cabinet was locked. He knelt down next to Finnerman's desk chair and prodded the upholstery underneath. He felt the underside of each desk drawer to see if anything were held there with tape. He felt *behind* the file cabinet where it didn't quite touch the wall.

He found nothing.

Think! Think!

He leaned, frustrated, with his fists pressed hard against the top of Finnerman's desk. He scanned the office again: the art on the walls, the vinyl potted plant in the corner, the open briefcase. He looked more closely at the bookshelf, tilting his head to read the titles of the books, journals, and technical manuals there. Phrases like "virtual imaging" and "laser holography" appeared again and again.

Of course, Finnerman was a computer engineer. It made sense for him to have these materials. Peter grabbed one journal after another and flipped through them. *Software design, realistic motion in computer game characters....*

"Hey!" whispered Jake. "While you're doing that, toss me his organizer. I want to see what this guy does with his time."

Peter grabbed the electronic organizer from the briefcase and lobbed it to Jake's waiting hands. The next journal Peter flipped through had a page corner folded down. The marked page contained an article entitled "Holographic Projection." An illustration of a complex diagram appeared there; a design for a camera or something. The caption read: *Design A for 3-D hologram projector.*

Peter replaced the journal and scanned through the shelf again. There were two copies of a book with something to do with holograms by an author named Hagerty. *Why two copies?* One was older, and the other had a plastic dust jacket and a tiny, numbered label on its spine. He flipped through the pages of the book, but it was too technical for him to follow.

"Now! He's coming!" hissed Jake.

Peter hurriedly replaced the book where he had found it. Jake tossed the organizer across the room to him and Peter laid it in the briefcase. He and Jake threw themselves into their seats just as Mr. Finnerman returned through the door.

"Sorry to keep you waiting, boys," he said. This time he sat awkwardly on the corner of his desk instead of taking the chair.

"Well," said Peter, "we won't take up any more of your time. We just wanted to pass along our thoughts." He and Jake got up to leave, and Peter made a show out of looking around at the office. "Boy," he said, "this sure is a nice office. What kind of work do you actually do here, Mr. Finnerman?"

The man took in a deep breath. He smiled, apparently grateful for the change in the conversation. "I work in the design of new computer systems—advanced video games, simulators, 3-D systems like virtual reality, things like that."

Peter nodded, still standing in front of Finnerman's desk. He tried to make his voice sound as innocent as possible. "3-D, huh? Do you do any work with holograms?"

The man's face went gray. A little gurgling sound came from his throat as he swallowed. "Holograms? Why do you ask?"

Peter smiled. "Oh, I was just discussing them with my father, who's an FBI agent." He looked straight into Finnerman's eyes. "I've learned a lot about holograms in the last few days, and I expect to learn a lot more." The businessman's hands were visibly trembling, and Peter clasped one in a firm handshake. He broadened his smile. "It's been a pleasure meeting you," he said.

He and Jake left the office.

When they left, Mr. Finnerman let out a breath and collapsed in his chair. A moment later he rose from his desk, looked down the hallway, and when he was sure that Peter and Jake were gone, he shut the door.

He hands were trembling so much by now that he could barely punch the numbers on the telephone.

"Yes?" said the voice on the other end.

"Roarke? This is Finnerman."

Finnerman could practically hear the scowl through the phone line. "You're not supposed to call here, Finnerman. Your part in this is finished. You've been paid well for your efforts so far, and you'll be paid a fair portion when I close the deal in Europe."

"This isn't about money," Finnerman hissed. "We have a problem. A couple of teenagers just wormed their way up to my office. They said they know the security guy is innocent."

"Teenagers? High school brats?"

Finnerman let out a deep sigh and shuddered. "Yes. And—one of them mentioned holograms."

"Now *that's* very interesting," Roarke finally said, his voice flat. "Do you believe," asked Roarke, "that these kids might prove to be a danger to us?"

"Yes," Finnerman said. "I—I'm not sure, but I think they might. One of them, the one who did all the talking, seemed real sure of himself. I tell you, Roarke, he knows something!"

"Well, then," said Roarke, and his voice sounded almost sad. "This really is quite unfortunate. I like to avoid these situations, but sometimes it just can't be helped. I suppose I'll have to use Mr. Krohg. Quickly,

Finnerman, find out what type of car your visitors are driving."

Finnerman turned and leaned near the window behind him. Two distant figures were climbing into an old red Volkswagen. He described the car to Roarke, and he heard Roarke giving terse instructions to another person. Then Roarke spoke again to Finnerman.

"The problem is solved," he announced. "I am in touch with Mr. Krohg via cell phone. He—well, he just happens to be near your office. He will take care of these pests."

Finnerman shuddered again. Mr. Krohg just *happened* to be near his office? Finnerman quickly realized why. Roarke must have ordered Mr. Krohg to keep *him*—Finnerman!—under surveillance. The monster was probably in a hotel room across the street, watching Finnerman with a telescope. Whatever tortures Krohg conceived against these kids, Finnerman realized, might just as easily befall him too, if he didn't watch his step and do exactly as Roarke told him.

But these were just kids! Could he just stand back now and say nothing?

No! Every muscle in Finnerman's body seemed to be trembling. "Is taking action…in our…in our best interest?" he stammered, his voice sounding far higher and weaker than he would have liked. "I mean, do we want to call that much attention to ourselves?"

Roarke snorted. "You know computers," he said. "Let *me* handle the people problems." He continued speaking

64 in a cool, sterile manner. "Finnerman, I've waited too long for this chance. I won't have the whole thing ruined because of a couple of high school kids. So *just shut up and do as I tell you!*" the voice growled. "And don't ever question me again."

The phone clicked loudly in Finnerman's ear as Roarke slammed down the receiver.

Bill Finnerman, vice president of new products for InterTel Microchips International, slumped into his desk chair and let his face fall into his hands. He had joined up with Roarke because of the lure of the money. Roarke had offered him incredible sums of money—more money than Finnerman would ever be able to spend, money enough for a mansion, for all the cars he wanted, for the women. He knew if he could just get that much money, he would finally become popular and important. Now the plan was going wrong, and Bill Finnerman—tall, fat, stoop-shouldered, and balding— might be complicit in a murder. *It just can't be helped,* Roarke had said.

A moan pushed from Finnerman's chest and caught in his throat.

"I can't *believe* what you did in there," Jake said, walking swiftly toward the car.

Peter looked at his still-quivering hand. "Actually, I can't believe it either! I think I really scared him."

Peter quickly rolled back the vinyl top of his convertible Beetle and they climbed inside. The car put-putted to life, and Peter rammed the stick shift into gear and drove out of the parking lot onto the street.

"Let's get back to my house and call Byte and Mattie right away," said Peter. "We all need to talk about this together."

Peter couldn't help but smile. Detective work, he decided, wasn't all that hard after all.

He didn't even notice the black Nissan Pathfinder that wove in and out of traffic and followed Peter's cherry red Volkswagen down the street.

chapter five

to get out of the crowded part of the city, Peter turned toward Old Shore Road. It was a narrow, two-lane highway that wound in a series of crazy switch-backs as it edged the cliffs overlooking Bugle Bay. Its path was treacherous, and most drivers preferred to take the new freeway that cut through the center of the city. But Peter liked to see the view from the highest part of the cliff, where he could look down across the marina as he drove and watch the water lapping at the rocks over two hundred feet below.

As the road twisted and began the steep climb, Peter downshifted because the engine started to strain.

It was then he noticed that the vehicle behind him seemed to be accelerating and drawing closer. He watched it grow larger in his mirror as it approached.

"Hey," he said, "that guy's getting a little too close."

It was the Pathfinder. Jake twisted around to look at it, and Peter studied it through the rearview mirror. He tried to see the face of the person who was driving, but the windshield was tinted too dark. The black vehicle closed in on the rear bumper of the Volkswagen, riding only inches away.

"That guy's crazy," said Jake. "Is he trying to pass us?"

Peter's heart beat faster. The rocky cliff face lay at his right. To his left was a narrow oncoming traffic lane, and beyond that the cliff's sweeping drop toward the bay and the rocks far below. He forced himself to concentrate on his driving.

"What does he think he's doing?" Jake said angrily. The Pathfinder nudged Peter's car, tapping it lightly. But the faster Peter drove to get away, the greater chance he had of losing control and crashing. As the cars climbed, the rocks and the bay dropped farther and farther below them.

"Look out," warned Jake, bracing himself against the seat and the dash. "Here he comes!"

The Pathfinder roared. It smacked hard against the rear engine hood of the Volkswagen. Peter felt his head snap forward and then back against the headrest.

"One more of those," Jake said, "and we can forget about driving away from this." He tried to calm Peter by making a joke. "You're the smart one. How is it you picked the one car ever made whose engine is in the back?"

The road curved again, and only Peter's familiarity with the road allowed him to make the turn. His brakes squealed and some gravel spit out from underneath the tires, skittering across the other lane and down the cliff face, but the tires held. Peter whipped the steering wheel around sharply and stomped on the accelerator.

Jake, still facing backward, wrapped his arms around the seat back for support. "Hang on!" he shouted. "He's coming in for another shot!"

Peter tightened his grip on the wheel to steady the Volkswagen's swerving. The Pathfinder roared and loomed larger in the mirror. Once again, the heavy sport vehicle rammed the tiny Volkswagen. The smaller car lurched forward, propelled by the impact, and Peter swerved wildly to avoid hitting an oncoming minivan. The Pathfinder struck again, and the Volkswagen grazed the cliff face. A spray of sparks leaped from the right front bumper where metal scraped against rock. But the Pathfinder was not finished yet. *Wham!* The truck hit them again.

"You can do this, Peter," Jake said. "Stay cool. You'll get us out of here."

And then it happened: The Pathfinder's bumper caught on the now-sprung engine hood of the Volkswagen. Locked together, the two vehicles shot toward the next curve in the road, dangerously close to having their momentum carry them across the narrow left lane and over the edge of the cliff. Peter could not stop or pull away. Hitched behind him was the Pathfinder, and just ahead of him was a one-hundred-sixty-foot drop.

"Hit your brakes!" yelled Jake. "You might be able to slow him down!"

Peter forced himself to remain calm. *No,* he thought. *I can't slow down a Pathfinder. It's too heavy. The accelerator. Hit the accelerator.* Peter jammed his foot down on the gas pedal once again. The engine whined, struggling to pull away. Peter heard the groan of metal twisting, then felt and heard a loud *snap* as the engine cover broke off the back of the Volkswagen and the smaller car pulled free. It leaped forward, and Peter was just able to steer toward the inside of the curve. In the mirror he saw the hood as it fell beneath the wheels of the swerving Pathfinder, crumpled like aluminum foil under the truck's weight, then tumbled off the cliff. The Pathfinder slowed, trying to regain control.

As the truck braked, Peter downshifted once again, zipped around the next curve, shifted back up into third, and pulled ahead, out of sight of the Pathfinder. For a moment, they were safe. The feeling of panic subsided, replaced by the rush of adrenaline. Peter ignored the wild pounding of his heart and analyzed the situation: *The Pathfinder is bigger and heavier than my car, and more powerful. But my car is smaller, lighter, and more maneuverable, which means that it can turn and accelerate more quickly than the Pathfinder. Best of all,* Peter reminded himself, *I know how to drive this road.*

Jake also had an idea. "Peter!" he shouted, the wind whistling around them. "Keep slowing down into the turns, then hit the gas hard when moving out of them. That'll put some distance between us and that monster, and it might even give us some room to find an escape."

Peter punched the gas and the Beetle shot forward, leaving the Pathfinder far behind. The engine, straining against the demands Peter was making of it, screamed with the pain of its efforts. Its whining was high pitched and desperate. But Peter knew that if he shifted up into fourth, the engine wouldn't have enough torque to accelerate on this road.

"I know where we can lose this guy!" Peter shouted back.

They pulled around another turn, and for a few moments the cliff face prevented the driver of the Pathfinder from seeing them. Peter slowed. Up ahead the road widened, and he knew there was a stand of tall, thick green bushes off to the side. The cliff was strange that way. It looked like mostly rock, but here and there, where rain and space allowed, large bushes had taken root.

He swung the Beetle off the road. Because of its small size, Peter managed to squeeze it in between the bushes and the cliff face. He knew the leaves would not cover the red car entirely, but the sun was beginning to angle low in the sky, and Peter hoped the shadows would give him added invisibility.

The boys waited tensely. Moisture from the leaves around them lightly spattered the Volkswagen's plaid upholstery. They tensed as they heard the Pathfinder's engine roaring louder. A moment later it tore right past them, kicking up dust and gravel as it rounded the curve.

Peter and Jake stared almost unbelieving through the branches as it passed. Neither boy looked at the other. Peter felt a tingling through his body as the numbing shock of the chase began to wear off, and he wondered if Jake had the same feeling.

"Are you all right?" he asked Jake.

Jake nodded. "Yeah."

"That was…scary."

Jake nodded again. "Yeah."

Any moment the driver of the Pathfinder could figure out what they had done and come back for them, so Peter and Jake didn't want to stay in the bushes any longer than necessary. After a few moments, Peter climbed out to take stock of the damage to his car and decided it would run. He wondered if he should go to the police first, in case they were still being followed, or just go to his house. His house was much closer, and he just wanted to get home, so he decided to go directly home and call the police from there.

"My folks are going to kill me when they see the car," he said.

"No kidding," said Jake, and he gave Peter a weak, wry smile. "It might have been easier on you if we had just driven this thing right off the cliff."

They arrived at Peter's house fifteen minutes later.

Byte and Mattie ran from the front steps to greet the arriving car.

"Whoa!" said Mattie, staring at the crumpled Volkswagen as Peter pulled into the garage.

The right front fender was badly scraped and dented. The engine hood was gone completely, lost somewhere in the rocks and water along the shore of Bugle Bay, and the rear bumper had sprung loose.

"Looks like you had an interesting afternoon."

"It gets more interesting," said Peter, closing the garage door so the car couldn't be seen from the street. "Come on."

Mattie looked over his shoulder at the garage as they headed back into the house. "I can't wait to hear this," he said.

They met in Peter's rec room. Mattie busied himself taking apart a stereo speaker. Peter knew it helped him think, so he didn't stop him. He only hoped one of his parents didn't walk in and see the mess.

"We didn't find anything much. Some magic, sleight of hand stuff that wasn't too promising," said Byte, who was sitting on the floor, typing furiously on her notebook computer. "Someone loaded a virus onto the one journal article I wanted to download from the Net, supposedly *the* major article on new developments in holograms. As far as I can tell, the virus didn't damage my computer, but I couldn't get to the article." She shivered.

"So I called the main Portland library and the librarian said they have the back issues of this journal on CD-ROM, but the disk had recently become *damaged*. They don't know how it got that way. I ordered a copy from the journal itself, but it'll take a while to get it."

"And to top it all off," Mattie said, "the books and magazine articles the library had about holograms were missing."

"Checked out, huh?" said Jake.

Mattie shook his head and glanced at Byte as he answered. "Not checked out. It looked like all the information was stolen. The pages of every article related to holograms that I found were ripped out of each magazine—Byte saw it too. It was very weird." He fidgeted with the speaker parts strewn about the floor. "The one book I was looking for," Mattie went on, "was a very new one I was sure would be useful. But it was missing. Not checked out, not on loan to another branch, just gone. And there was a loose magnetic strip lying on the shelf where the book was supposed to be."

Peter's mind slowly drifted away from the conversation. He thought back to the book and journals he'd seen in Finnerman's office. One copy of the book had been covered by a clear dust jacket with a numbered label—it had come from a library.

"What do you mean?" asked Jake.

"When I used to work at the school library," Mattie explained, "we glued a magnetic strip into the spine of each book for security. The strip sets off an alarm if

74 someone leaves before an employee has dragged it across the de-magnetizer. Someone was covering his tracks. He didn't want to check out the books or magazines, because then his name would be in the system."

"From what I've found on-line," Byte said, "it sounds like this book is absolutely the best source for comprehensive hologram information. The author's name is—"

"—Hagerty," said Peter.

Byte stopped typing and gaped at Peter as he mulled over this new information.

"How the heck d'you know that?" Jake demanded.

Peter looked at the others as though he had just noticed that they were in the room. "Oh—the book you're talking about was in Finnerman's office. I saw it today at InterTel."

"The guy you went to see at InterTel has this very book—the *stolen* book?" Byte asked.

Peter was only halfway involved in the conversation, his mind racing as he tried to remember what he had seen. He managed a nod. "Yeah, it was a library book. I saw it. Plus another copy. I even looked through one."

"Hey, wait a minute," said Jake. "That library book might tie into what I saw in Finnerman's daily planner. There were two references from last week that said 'library.'"

"So the library and Net materials on holograms were either contaminated with a virus, damaged, or stolen," Byte said slowly. "Finnerman was at the library, and he has one of the missing items. Why? What is Finnerman up to?"

Peter shook his head. "I don't know. Remember, Finnerman freely told us he works on virtual reality projects, so holograms are probably part of his job, too. Therefore he has every reason to have materials on holograms in his office. But we know he went to the library recently, and we know he stole a book while he was there—one he already has a copy of—instead of checking it out. It certainly would fit that for some reason he's responsible for these *other* damaged or missing materials as well."

"But he has access to materials on holograms. Why would he steal them?" Mattie asked, puzzled.

"I don't know. He seems to be hiding *something*, and it's connected to holograms." Peter rubbed his eyes. After the car chase along the cliff's edge, he was rattled and finding it hard to put all the facts together. He leaned back into the couch. "All right, let's back up. After talking to Mr. Blair, I wondered if holograms might have something to do with this robbery. As Mr. Blair says, solid objects don't just disappear."

Mattie nodded. "But holograms *aren't* solid. Computer chips like the 1286dx that disappeared *are*."

Peter smiled tiredly. "Exactly. The only way it would work is if the person who stole the chip *somehow* set up a hologram in the display case *in place of* the chip, not reflecting the chip itself. Everyone would see the hologram and think the chip was still there, but it would be gone. I just don't know how the thief would do it."

"Finnerman certainly knows about holograms. But why would he steal his own company's chip?" Jake asked.

"Who knows? But he was very nervous in his office." Peter paused. "And look what happened afterward."

Peter's remark hung in the air like a thundercloud.

Jake gave a little nod. "Yeah," he said quietly. "I can still see the gravel spraying out from under your tires and shooting over the cliff."

He wasn't the only member of the group who was nervous. All of them were beginning to realize the seriousness of this investigation. Someone seemed to be trying to scare them away from hologram information. Flesh-and-blood hands had been guiding the steering wheel of the Pathfinder that had tried to shove Jake and Peter over the cliff. Peter, Byte, Jake, and Mattie were amateur detectives, but they were dealing with professional criminals.

Peter looked at their faces and realized they were all more than a little frightened. Some uncomfortable questions flashed in Peter's mind: *Have we already gone too far? Are we in over our heads?*

It was almost completely dark outside now. A streetlamp cast its glow through the window frame, streaking their faces with alternating lines of shadow and light. They had been so caught up in their conversation that no one had thought to turn a light on.

Peter decided that, since he had gotten them into this, he had to be the one to voice the doubts: "So," he said, "do we want to keep working on this?"

The others' heads whipped around to look at him.

Jake bounced his Superball twice against the wall. It vanished into his palm when he caught it. He paused, then admitted, "I like Mattie's grandfather, and I know he didn't steal the chip. It might be dangerous, but if we can help him, I'd like to try."

Byte nodded. "I agree. Besides, square pegs stick together. I'm not going anywhere."

They all turned and looked at Mattie, and even in the dark Peter could see the younger boy's face harden. A moment passed before Mattie spoke. "I'm scared," he said. "But I love my grandfather, and I'd sure hate myself if we stopped now."

It was getting late, and the group was tired. "Okay." Peter nodded. "I'll talk to my dad about our theory. Maybe he'll have some ideas." He looked at the others. "We'd better tell the police, too."

Mr. Braddock's footsteps on the front porch were only a little less frightening, Peter thought, than the oncoming roar of the Pathfinder. The more Peter considered the wrecked Volkswagen outside and the hours his father had put into restoring it, getting run over by a sport utility vehicle seemed like it might have been a quicker and more merciful death.

Nick Braddock walked into the den, his jacket slung over his arm and a newspaper clutched in his hand. In his other hand was his briefcase, and Peter nervously watched him snap its latches open and lay the briefcase on the coffee table. He removed some papers, flicked on the light, and sat down on the couch to read. "Hey, Pete," he said, "how was your day?"

"Interesting," said Peter. He remembered reading once about an ancient Oriental curse: *May your days be interesting.* Well, recently his days had been *very* interesting, and Peter could only hope that they would be a little less interesting in the future.

"I would guess so," said Mr. Braddock. "I saw your car when I pulled in. Are you all right?"

"Yeah."

"What happened?"

Peter struggled with that one. If he told his father everything, as he had told his friends he would, he might get some help in solving the case. But his dad might also see the possible danger Peter was in and put an end to the investigation. The trick was to give his dad an answer that was truthful and yet so simple it didn't encourage further questions. "I was rear-ended," he said carefully. "No one was hurt, but I'm sorry about the car. I'll call the insurance company first thing in the morning—they were already closed when we got home—then take the car to the shop and get an estimate. Okay?" That was a good response, Peter thought. Not only did he answer the question without lying, he had also managed to change the subject.

Or so he thought.

"You got the name and license of the other driver?" asked his father.

"No, sir," said Peter. He didn't often call his father "sir," but now seemed a pretty good time. "It was sort of a hit-and-run."

"Ah," said Mr. Braddock, "so of course you've already called the police and filed an accident report."

Peter was sure his face turned stark white. "Um, no sir," he said. "I guess I got involved talking with my friends and I forgot to do that."

His father nodded. "The phone's over there," he said flatly. "Call them now. They'll send an officer over. I'm looking forward to hearing every detail."

Mr. Braddock went back to his paperwork while Peter called the police. The dispatcher said an officer would be over in about an hour. Peter sighed. Maybe he would get lucky. Maybe his father would get distracted by his work and stop asking questions.... But that was a foolish thought indeed. Criminals who figured they could outsmart Nick Braddock only trapped themselves in the end. The same rule applied to teenage sons.

"Where's your mom?" asked Mr. Braddock.

"She left a note that she was grocery shopping."

Peter's father nodded, and Peter squirmed a bit. He was always a little wary when his father engaged in small talk;

more often than not, the conversation had a deeper motive behind it.

"So Peter," continued his dad, "what are you doing with your time now that you're out of school?"

Peter froze, his suspicions mounting. His father had asked the question in such an offhand way. It almost had to be a trap. Mr. Braddock had a special way of asking questions: He would speak so lightly and easily that Peter would often find himself answering before he realized how much trouble he was getting himself into.

"Oh," he said, "I've been hanging out with Jake and Byte and Mattie, mostly. Not doing anything special." *Is that a lie?* Peter felt his face flush and thought he'd better hurry up and fill in with something. "Um—Jake and I went downtown today." *Ouch! I'm saying too much. The less I say, the better off I am.*

"I see." Mr. Braddock set down the sheaf of papers. "I don't suppose, then, that you and your friends are trying to solve the disappearance of the chip, are you?"

Well, there it was. Peter slumped in his chair. There was no point in hiding anything now. "Yeah," he said, "I guess we are. How did you know?"

"Until now, I didn't. I just suspected." Mr. Braddock set the papers on the table and leaned back into the sofa cushions. "Does the damage to your car have anything to do with your investigation?"

Peter had to think about that one. He took in a deep breath and let it out slowly. "Probably. I can't say for sure that there's a connection, but it seems likely." He told his father about the trip to InterTel, about the climb up Old Shore Road, and about the Pathfinder ramming him. Nick Braddock listened calmly, but Peter saw the muscles tensing in his father's neck.

"Looks like you've stepped on somebody's toes."

"Hmm?"

"You must be coming close to learning something," Mr. Braddock said. "You made someone nervous enough to come after you. In my work, I take it as a compliment when someone comes after me. It means I'm doing my job well." He frowned. "But law enforcement is hardly a job for teenagers. It's too dangerous. I'm afraid your investigation ends here and now, Peter. Whatever you've learned, you'll have to share it with the local PD and let them deal with it."

Peter knew his father was right. He had not wanted to think about such things, but after the chase on the cliff today he had no choice. He had to think about who these people were and what else they might do to him and his friends if he continued.

But then, Peter wondered, *what about Mattie's grandfather? Doesn't he deserve some consideration?*

"Dad," said Peter, "can we at least do a little innocent snooping? Some research, maybe? We'll stay out of trouble, and we won't go near any suspects. I promise."

Mr. Braddock took a deep breath.

"And," Peter added quickly, "anything we find out we'll report immediately to you or to Lieutenant Decker at the police station. Fair enough?"

Mr. Braddock nodded with reluctance. He pointed his index finger at Peter. "Information gathering only," he warned. "Nothing more. And from now on, you keep your distance from anything even remotely dangerous."

Peter grinned. "It's a deal."

Mr. Braddock then reached into his briefcase and pulled out a file folder. He opened the folder, and Peter watched him spread out three eight-by-ten photographs on the coffee table. The black-and-whites each showed the figure of a man. On the back of each photo were printed the man's vital statistics—his height, weight, fingerprints, aliases, and known associates. "Peter," he said, "I want you to take a look at these. I've been doing a little snooping myself—unofficially, of course—and I've brought home some things that might interest you." He turned the photographs around so Peter could see them better. "These are some thieves the bureau has been trying to track down. Any one of them has the brains and ability to steal the 1286dx."

Peter leaned over and looked at the photos. The first was a little blurry, and it had a graininess to it that suggested that it was a blown up detail from another photograph. The image was of a heavyset man with a scruffy beard and loose, jowly cheeks. The man had a scar below his left eye and a thick, narrow mustache. His arm was raised, and he pointed an Uzi directly at the camera.

"That's Ackbar Mohammad Hassad. Nasty guy—I've had more than one run-in with him. His specialty is stealing world-famous pieces of jewelry and ransoming them back to their owners, but he dabbles in other large thefts as well. The agent who took this photo barely got away."

The next photo showed a tiny man with frail, delicate features in a café. Just a few wisps of hair remained on his balding head, and the skin around his eyes sagged. His eyes, Peter noticed, were scanning the surroundings the way a lion might scan a herd of zebras, looking for the frailest, the weakest.

"Don't let this one's age fool you," said Mr. Braddock. "His name is Sven Larsen. Sixty-seven years old. He looks harmless, but he's as deadly as an old grizzly bear. Not only is he a master thief, but he's also a weapons expert, Peter, and a weapon is anything he can get his hands on. He's wanted for several murders; the most recent involved slitting a man's throat with the edge of a playing card."

Peter shuddered and whistled. He studied Larsen's photo for another moment, then turned his attention to the third. This one was of a tall, thin man with a high forehead and thick, silvery hair. The man was seated in an audience, and from the intricate, decorative carving on the walls of the room, Peter guessed he was in an old European theater. Strangely, the man looked at the camera as though he knew someone was taking his picture. His smile seemed to challenge his pursuer.

Peter's father grunted. "I guess we all have a nemesis," he said. "Well, you're looking at mine. I've spent half my years in the bureau hunting down this man, and I've never even seen him in person. I've been close to finding him, but he's always been one step ahead. He has lots of names—sometimes he's Grayson Ellis, sometimes Winslowe McKay—but most often he likes to call himself Malcolm Roarke. Nobody knows his real name. He likes to steal valuable inventions, especially new ones. Then he sells to the highest bidder, usually for millions. He's a bad one, kiddo. He'll do anything to protect what he's got. You see him, you stay away. Got it?"

Peter looked closely at the photograph of Malcolm Roarke, and the eyes in the photo glared back at him. Peter imagined the photo hanging on the wall of a room, the eyes following him as he walked past. A chill started at the base of his spine and spread up his back and across his shoulders. After a moment the tingling reached his fingers, and Peter dropped the photo onto the desk. "I understand, Dad," he said. "I'll be careful."

He laid down on the couch after his father left, the photograph still on the table next to him. He reached up and turned off the light. Peter wanted to think, and it helped if the room was dark. More than anything else, he wanted to sort through the events of the day. *Finnerman at InterTel…the library book…the Pathfinder….*

Strangely, even after the danger on Old Shore Road, it was the photograph of Roarke that shook Peter the most. The moment he saw the picture—that face with the eerily charming yet daring smile—an alarm had sounded within him. Peter envisioned the face again and shuddered.

The key to the mystery was Finnerman; Peter was certain of that much. Finnerman had the stolen library book. He knew about holograms, and as vice-president at InterTel, he was the person who had lent the chip to the museum.

Peter tiredly closed his eyes. His mind drifted, and he saw himself in Finnerman's office. He watched himself reach for the book and flip hurriedly through its pages. He saw the illustration, and the caption beneath the illustration seemed to rise up in bold letters: *Design A for three-dimensional hologram projector.*

Hologram *projector?*

Peter bolted upright, his eyes now wide open. A 3-D projector of some kind—that had to be the answer! If the thief was able to create a fake, 3-D copy of the chip instead of merely reflecting it as Mr. Blair's hologram toy had done…if the thief projected a 3-D image of the chip that was independent of the real chip, he could take the real chip away and everyone would think it was still there! The only way the theft would have worked is with a hologram projector.

But where could the thief hide a projector? In the wall of the museum? No, the wall was too far away from the display stand, and it would have been too hard to cut a hole in the wall to make a place for the projector. In the ceiling? Nope—same problems. Wherever the projector was, Peter decided, it would have to be somewhere very close to the display stand where the chip had disappeared.

And then it came to him. Peter leaned back and smiled.

He felt satisfied with his day's work, but there was one more job to do. Peter reached in his wallet for the business card Lieutenant Decker had given him and dialed the number. Though a uniformed officer would be at Peter's house shortly to take his accident report, Peter knew it was best to speak directly to Decker.

"Police. This is Lieutenant Decker, Robbery Division." The lieutenant's words were muffled, as though his mouth were full of food.

"Lieutenant," said Peter, "this is Peter Braddock. About the microchip robbery at the museum? Can you meet me there tomorrow morning at ten o' clock? I have an idea about how the chip may have been stolen."

He heard Decker's lips smack. "And how's that?"

"I can't explain over the phone," said Peter. "I have to show you."

The detective paused, then sighed. "All right, kid," he said, "but this had better not be a waste of time. I'm really busy over here."

"I don't think you'll be disappointed," said Peter. "In fact, I think it's going to be a very interesting morning."

Peter hung up the phone and smiled, satisfied that they were closer than ever to catching the true thief of the 1286dx. He had already forgotten that there were many different *kinds* of interesting, some pleasant and some not so pleasant.

Peter, Byte, Jake, and Mattie arrived at the museum precisely at ten A.M. Lieutenant Decker was waiting for them. "This'd better be good, kid," he said.

"I believe it will be, sir," said Peter. "Would you follow us, please?" The teenagers led the lieutenant into the main display room of the museum. The marble display stand that had housed the 1286dx still stood in the center of the room. Around the stand was a police barrier, heavy yellow tape preventing people from accidentally destroying evidence.

"Have your men examined this display stand?" asked Peter.

Decker scowled. "Of course. What's on your mind?"

"I'll show you," said Peter. "Jake, would you give me a hand here?"

Jake and Peter positioned themselves on either side of the display stand. They were careful not to touch the parts of the case that were covered with fingerprint dust.

"On three," said Peter. "One…two…*three!*" The boys lifted up the Plexiglas cube that rested on top of the display stand and set it on the floor. "Now," said Peter eagerly, "we can get a better idea of what really happened here. Lieutenant, you might want to have a look at this."

Peter was standing over the cube-shaped marble base, looking down at the bowl that had served to display the computer chip. The bowl looked a little like a black, metallic Frisbee. "Look," he said, "right there."

In the center of the bowl was a hole about half an inch wide.

"Awright, so there's a hole there. We saw it. Nothing is in there," said Decker. "What's this all about?"

The bowl was set into the marble with heavy screws. "I can tell you," said Peter, "but we'll need to remove this bowl. Mattie?"

Decker hesitated. He wasn't exactly in the mood to let some teenager take apart a whole museum screw by screw. Then he waved his hand. "Ah, you've already dragged me out here," he said. "What's the harm? Worst that can happen is you four make fools of yourselves."

Mattie came forward. Attached to his belt was a leather pouch containing a multi-tool. He pulled it out, tugging at it until he found a screwdriver tip that suited him.

Someone had built the display fairly recently. The screws were clean, not dirty or rusty, and they twisted out with little effort. Mattie dropped one after another into his palm. A moment later he lifted the bowl from the marble base, revealing a hollow opening. Peter stared into it, but he saw nothing. The display stand was empty. His eyebrows creased into a frown.

"I told you, kid," said Decker. "We already looked inside the display. It's a dead end."

Peter bit his lip. *Something's not right,* he told himself. *There's just no other way to make it work. It* has *to be here!* He thought for a moment longer.

"Jake," he said, "help me move this stand."

The marble base was much heavier than the Plexiglas cube. Peter and Jake braced their shoulders against it and slid it two feet across the floor.

"Hey," said Decker. "What are you doing there?"

Moving the display stand revealed a missing tile in the floor and a hole where the tile had been. In the opening was a small piece of metal shaped in a shallow bowl, and it was as bright and reflective as a shiny new mirror. *Just like Mr. Blair's hologram toy,* mused Peter. In the center of this mirror was another hole.

"Don't touch that!" said the lieutenant. He pulled a pair of rubber gloves from his pocket and tossed them to Peter. "Wear these. I don't want you spoiling any fingerprints."

Peter nodded. "Right." He pulled on the gloves and lifted the mirror out of the floor, careful to touch only the edges, and handed it to the lieutenant. Decker wrapped the mirror in a handkerchief.

"We're not finished yet," said Peter. He looked into the dark opening. As he'd suspected, something else was beneath, hidden in the shadows. Peter reached down and grasped the heavy object cased in thick metal. He pulled it up and set it on the edge of the opening.

"I don't believe it," sputtered Decker. "We took the top off the display—did all kinds of tests on the base—but it just looked like a normal hunk of marble. There didn't seem to be any point in checking further...." His words trailed off to an annoyed grumbling.

The object looked like a video camera with a metal tube protruding from the top. At the end of this tube was a glass lens. "If I'm right," said Peter, "this is how the thief stole the 1286dx."

"What is it?" asked the lieutenant.

"It's a hologram projector. It creates a three-dimensional image."

Peter found a switch on the side of the projector and flicked it a couple of times. Nothing happened. He flicked the switch a couple more times, but with no success. No light. No whirring of tiny motors. None of the electronic wizardry Peter expected. *What's the problem?* Peter puzzled, his frustration and embarrassment mounting.

"Why isn't it working?" Mattie asked.

Peter racked his brain, then he turned the projector over. He popped open a small lid on the bottom, looked inside, and then glanced around the room. His eyes fell on the new security guard's belt.

"May I borrow your flashlight?" he asked the guard.

When the guard handed it over, Peter unscrewed the end of it and poured out the flashlight's batteries into his hand. He removed the batteries from the projector and popped in the new ones. When he flipped the switch again, the machine hummed.

Peter fitted the mirror back onto the projector and waited tensely. In a long moment the 1286dx chip began to appear in the air. Peter ran his finger through it as if it weren't even there—which, in fact, it wasn't. "It's a mirage," Peter said, "a three-dimensional… projection."

Decker nodded. He understood. "Well, darn if that isn't the most amazing thing I ever saw. Kid, you did real good."

"There would have to be a digital image of the 1286dx recorded on a computer chip inside the projector," said Byte.

"Awesome!" said Mattie. "And a laser projects the image to a curved mirror or series of mirrors, and you get a perfect 3-D hologram!" He stared at the projector. "I wish I could take a look inside that thing…."

"This means that the real chip was stolen long before that day we saw it disappear," said Byte.

"Right," said Peter. "Whoever stole the chip put in this hologram projector so that no one would know that the chip was missing."

"And the hologram vanished because its *batteries* ran out?" asked Jake incredulously.

Peter grinned. "Right."

Decker walked slowly over to Peter, pondering all this new information. "Okay, then," he finally said, more to himself than to Peter. "Whoever set up that gadget had to be able to get into the display case without being noticed. He had to shut off the laser alarm system, and he had to get close enough to see the real chip so he could make that—whadjacallit—hologram. All of those ideas still point to the old man."

"But," noted Peter, "the thief also had to know enough about hologram technology to build this projector."

Decker nodded reluctantly. Clearly Peter's uncovering of the projector complicated matters for him.

"Finnerman's involved," said Peter. "You have to talk to Bill Finnerman at InterTel."

Decker scowled. "Finnerman? What's he got to do with all this? I've spoken with the guy, and he's real embarrassed about the theft."

"He's a book thief!" said Mattie.

"Yeah," said Jake, "and he acts really *nervous*."

Peter and the others surrounded the lieutenant and began talking all at once. Decker raised his hands and waved for everybody to stop.

"Awright, awright, *awright*," he said. "Just one of you talk." He pointed a finger at Peter. "You, kid. Tell me what the heck's going on here."

Peter looked at the others, gathered his thoughts, and took a deep breath. "Well," he said, "here's what we know." He started by telling Decker of the computer virus and the missing materials from the library. He told him how he had found and examined the book and seen the plans for the projector. He told him how nervous Finnerman had seemed, and he described, in great detail, the trip along Old Shore Road and the attack from the Pathfinder. Peter could tell he was not making much headway with the man. Decker scratched at his day-old growth of beard and waited for Peter to finish.

"So kid," he said, "how do you figure Finnerman, if he's the thief, got into the museum to set up that little projector right in front of everybody?"

Peter shrugged. "I don't know."

"And how did he get past the alarm system?"

"I don't know that either."

"And what about this Pathfinder? Unless you think Finnerman himself was driving it, which don't seem too likely, there's a whole other can of worms to deal with."

Peter shook his head, lost for an answer.

Decker reached into his pocket and took out the tin of aspirin. "And one more thing. Why do you suppose a guy who works for InterTel, a guy who makes more in a year than I make in three, a guy who took the heat from his bosses when the chip disappeared, would want to steal the dumb thing in the first place?"

Peter gulped. "I—well—I guess I haven't figured out everything yet."

Decker nodded. "Look, kid," he said. "You almost got yourself and your friend killed. Leave police work to the police, awright? And as for the story you told me, you got me interested, but you ain't got me convinced."

"What do I have to do?" asked Peter.

Decker popped two aspirin into his mouth and grimaced at the taste. "You gotta convince me."

Bill Finnerman struggled to get into his apartment. He balanced a pepperoni pizza in one hand, carried his briefcase in the other, dangled a plastic bag containing two *Star Wars* videos from one pinkie finger and held his keys in his teeth.

It took him a moment to untangle himself and get inside.

Before he ran the videos he relaxed on the couch and flipped on the evening news. The TV reporter was standing next to a man with thinning hair and a large, reddish nose. The man was wearing a shoulder holster.

"Today," the commentator said, "a breakthrough in the investigation of the science museum theft."

Finnerman was balancing a large, greasy slice of pizza on his fingertips, but when he heard the reporter's words the slice slipped from his fingers and landed upside down on his shirt.

"Oh no," he groaned, but he wasn't referring to the dropped pizza.

The red-nosed man—a police investigator—held up a plastic evidence bag containing a very familiar object. "This," he said, "is a hologram projector. The thief who stole the 1286dx used it to fool people into believing that the chip was still in the museum, when actually it had already been stolen. Examining this piece of equipment will help us locate the real thief."

Finnerman swallowed. Two days ago, when he had tried to slip into the museum and retrieve the projector, the security guard had almost seen him. Finnerman had known that someone would eventually find the device, but he had fooled himself into thinking it would be much later, when he was safely out of the country.

The news announcer smiled. "And how did you discover this projector?"

The detective grimaced. Clearly he was not comfortable answering questions on television. "Uh—we got a tip." The detective raised his hand to silence the news announcer's next question. "Sorry, pal. For the source's protection, we're not revealing any names."

Finnerman threw the slice of pizza back into the box and dabbed at his shirt with a napkin. Then he rushed to the phone. He picked it up, began punching in a number, then slammed the phone back down on its cradle. *I'm not supposed to call him. He told me never to call him again. If I call him, he'll be really mad, but if I don't call him he might be even madder.*

Finnerman paced around the room a couple of times. *So do I call him or not? I don't know. What's the worst he could do to me?* A high-pitched, nervous laugh escaped from him. Finnerman had met Roarke's "friend" Mr. Krohg, and that one meeting was enough to convince Finnerman that there was probably no limit to the *worst* Roarke could do.

But sometimes fate reaches in and snatches a decision right out of a person's hands. At that moment the telephone rang.

Then it rang a second time.

Malcolm Roarke drummed his fingers on the arm of his leather chair. A cloud of blue smoke rose to the ceiling as Roarke puffed on his pipe. In front of Roarke, spread open on the antique table, was the evening newspaper. The picture of the hologram projector was exceptionally clear. From fifteen feet away, the television set flickered. Roarke listened as a detective explained, in marvelous detail, the method by which Roarke and Finnerman had disguised the theft of the 1286dx. Oh, some details were missing; the detective hadn't yet figured out everything, but it was clear that he soon would. *Apparently*, Roarke thought, *Finnerman's friends are as dangerous as I thought.* Roarke's eyes narrowed, and he took another puff on his pipe.

The phone rang a third time.

He heard a click, followed by the hiss of an answering machine. The voice of that idiot, Finnerman—who had failed in the simplest task, removing the hologram projector from the museum floor—came on and sounded, well, just like one would expect an idiot to sound.

Hi, this is Bill. I can't come to the phone right now, so wait for the beep....

Roarke waited with what he considered to be extraordinary patience. He was angry, but he was not angry at those teenagers. Apparently, they were worthy foes. Roarke could almost admire their intelligence and savvy.

As Roarke heard the beep, his lips spread into a tight, thin smile, and he spoke in a calm tone. "Hello, Finnerman," he said. "You know who this is. You recognize my voice. I know you are home, so pick up the telephone before I send Mr. Krohg over to *wrap the cord around your neck!*"

There was another click, the tape machine made a series of beeps, and a voice came on the line. "Um—hello?"

"Finnerman, you have failed me."

The only reply was silence.

Roarke sighed, and a whiff of blue smoke escaped his lips and circled his head. "Finnerman, you removed the mirrors from the display case, but you *failed to remove the projector from the floor!* How could you have been so stupid?"

There was a long pause, and the answer was just what Roarke had suspected: "There—there wasn't time. The guard...he was...."

"Idiot!" shouted Roarke, then his tone changed as he thought through his current problem. "Hmmm. It seems Mr. Krohg has failed me as well. It's just as I thought. These teenagers—these children!—are far too clever for their own good. Far too clever for *our* own good. Understand?"

The voice on the other end of the phone sank to a whisper: "Yes."

"We cannot afford mistakes. We cannot let children interfere. Now that they have succeeded in exposing our methods, I suspect we'll be hearing from them again. I will contact Mr. Krohg. Next time, he will not fail."

Roarke thought he heard Finnerman gasp.

"However," continued Roarke, "you will have to take some steps to protect yourself. I expect that since you were careless enough to leave the projector in the display case, you probably also left something in the projector that will lead the police to you—like fingerprints. It will take them several days to complete the laboratory tests. So for the remainder of the week, you will continue to report to work. You will go into your computer system at work and destroy all the files connecting you with the 1286dx, then write a virus to use up all existing memory so the FBI cannot rebuild the files. Then, if you want to stay out of prison long enough to enjoy the money we will get, you will have to disappear. Find a hotel room somewhere and hide for a while under a phony name. Later, get out of the country. You may travel wherever you wish, though I would advise against trying to return to the United States."

Finnerman was sobbing now. Roarke could hear the weeping. It was, he thought, a terrible show of weakness. *But,* Roarke thought, *I will try to be forgiving this time. Perhaps working with Mr. Krohg will toughen Finnerman up.*

Finnerman let the receiver drop to the cradle. His hand was shaking. *Krohg. He's sending Krohg after those defenseless kids again. Dear God....*

Finnerman tried to imagine what Krohg might do, but the images were so horrible he had to put them out of his mind. Instead, he thought about something equally horrible: prison. Roarke was right. Those kids had found the hologram projector, and Finnerman knew they suspected *him* of building it. It was a sure bet they could lead the police to him.

He didn't have much time.

Finnerman trudged into his bedroom. He looked at the dark, sumptuous comforter on his bed, the one he had paid six hundred dollars for because the salesperson said it would lend an air of "casual elegance" to his "bedroom ensemble." He stared at the Salvador Dali lithograph hanging on his wall, art he had never liked or understood but whose colors, the decorator had said, complemented the comforter. He took a deep breath and let it out slowly. Then he shook his head. When Bill Finnerman looked at his apartment, all he now saw was a jumble of material things that seemed to belong to someone else. None of his expensive possessions had ever given him even an instant of happiness.

Finnerman pulled a large duffel bag out of his closet and tossed in a couple of pairs of pants. Then he walked over to his dresser and began flipping through the shirts in one of the drawers. As he pulled out several button-downs, he heard a rustle of papers. There, in the bottom of the drawer beneath a few scattered letters from his mother, he found a photograph. He brought it out into the dimming light from outside. The picture was of himself as a boy—a pudgy, smiling, gap-toothed nine-year-old in his wrinkled Cub Scout uniform. Finnerman gazed at the photo, and time moved slowly around him. The pizza grew cold on the table. The videos remained in their cases. The TV flickered with snow. And Finnerman, his breathing ragged and labored, sat on the edge of his bed in the dark room, clutching the photograph to his chest.

seven

We need a plan," said Peter.

He raised the binoculars again and looked for his "subject"; that was the word that his dad used when he was following someone. Right now Peter's subject was Bill Finnerman. The InterTel offices were directly across the street, and they came into focus when Peter turned the binoculars' adjustment knob.

"What do you have in mind?" asked Jake. Peter handed him the spyglasses, and Jake again took his turn looking through them. Byte would get them next, and then Mattie. It wasn't that they needed the binoculars all that much—to tell the truth, they could see just as easily without them—but Mattie insisted that they bring them along. They *were* spying, after all, he reminded them. And how can one spy without binoculars?

"I hope something happens soon," said Mattie. "I'm getting hungry again."

Byte rolled her eyes. "You already ate all my onion rings."

They had been sitting at this table outside of Burger Express for two hours waiting for Mr. Finnerman to do something exciting, or even mildly interesting, but Finnerman had disappointed them. If he hadn't left the building for lunch, they might not even have known he was there.

"This is boring," said Mattie.

Yes, Peter thought, *it is.*

The problem, Peter realized, was that Finnerman didn't *have* to do anything to help them. Finnerman was playing it cool, so cool that Peter believed he and his friends could wait for days and never see anything that might prove that Finnerman was involved in the theft of the chip.

"We have to force his hand," said Peter. "We have to somehow push him into doing something dumb. Scare him."

Jake smiled. "I like the sound of this already," he said. "What's the plan?"

The more Peter thought about Finnerman, the more certain he was that a scare tactic would work. After all, when they had visited Finnerman in his office and Peter mentioned holograms, Finnerman started to sweat. Peter had thought the man might turn into a puddle on the floor right in front of him.

"Let me get this straight," said Byte. "You want to shake this guy up, and you're looking for a way to do it?"

"Exactly," said Peter.

He watched Byte as she tilted her head slightly and pursed her lips. This expression, too, would go down in Peter's list of things that were cute about Byte.

She nodded to herself as if to say, *Yeah, this will work.* "Can you get me his phone number?" she asked.

"Sure." Peter reached into his wallet and removed the business card he had taken from Finnerman's desk. It showed the number for Finnerman's private office. "What are you going to do?" he asked.

A smile played across Byte's face. "You'll see," she said, and she held out her hand. "Anyone got thirty-five cents I can borrow?"

Bill Finnerman sat at his desk, his fingers trembling over the keyboard. *That police lieutenant calling me every day, reporters asking nosy questions, Krohg spying on me.... I just have to survive until the end of the week,* he thought, erasing his computer files one by one. *Anyone could do it.*

His head fell forward and thumped against the top of his desk. His entire body trembled. *I can't do it,* he thought.

Last night, when he finally slept, he dreamed of diving into an ocean of hundred-dollar bills. The bills formed a tidal wave, drowning him as they rustled like dying leaves over his head. Finnerman had awakened to the sound of his own screams.

104 The phone rang, and he finally answered it. "Bill Finnerman."

The female voice that came over the wire was very deep, very authoritative. She did not bother to introduce herself.

"I know who you are, Finnerman," she began. "I know what you've done, and I can prove it."

Finnerman gulped. "I—I don't know what you're talking about," he stammered. "You must have the wrong number."

"Don't toy with me, Finnerman," said the voice. "You want me to keep your dirty little secret? I'll be happy to. For one million dollars. That's a small price to pay for staying out of jail, wouldn't you say? By five o' clock today, Finnerman—or I go to the police," The voice hissed in his ear. "Understand?"

Finnerman's stomach felt queasy. He found he barely had the strength to speak. "Yes, yes," he croaked, "I understand completely. But how will I find you?"

There was a pause. "You won't have to," said the voice. "I'll find *you*."

Byte hung up the pay phone and coughed a couple of times. "I don't know how much longer I could have done that voice."

"You were great," Jake said.

"You could have fooled *me*," Peter said admiringly.

He turned his attention to Mattie. "Okay. It's time for Part B of Byte's plan," he said. "Are you sure you're up to it?"

Mattie grinned. "Piece of cake."

Byte took a small pad of paper from her purse, tore off a page, and scribbled a note. She signed the note with Peter's circle and square emblem, folded the paper in half, then handed it to Mattie. "You know where you're going?"

"Sure," he said. "No sweat. I'll be back here before anyone even knows I was in the building."

Mattie sounded braver than he felt. He stuck the note into his pocket, took a deep breath, and walked across the street.

This isn't that hard, he told himself. *You do this kind of thing at school all the time.* A voice inside him reminded him that school hallways did not have reception desks and security guards, but Mattie tried to ignore those differences. The plan required that he get up to Finnerman's office without being seen, so he would just have to figure out a way to accomplish that goal.

He crossed the street and knelt behind a tall bush just outside InterTel's glass lobby door. The receptionist was sitting at her desk, working at her computer. Mattie took a moment to study the lobby. The good news was that there was no security guard in sight. The bad news was that he had twenty feet of open floor he would have to cross without the receptionist seeing him.

Mattie closed his eyes and shook his head. Peter had done so well in figuring out how the chip had been stolen. Byte had been wonderful in her phone call to Finnerman. Mattie did not want to be the first member of the group to fail under pressure. And his grandfather needed him.

A few moments later, a group of three businessmen approached the door and entered the building. They were chatting loudly about a baseball game they had watched on TV the night before, and none of them noticed the small fourteen-year-old boy who slipped in behind them. Mattie walked lightly and kept close to the last member of the group. When they approached the reception desk, he walked around and behind the men, circling past the desk; and while they were smiling and trying their hardest to flirt with the receptionist, he crept down the hallway toward the staircase. If he used the elevator someone might see him, and he risked having to explain his presence.

Mattie was out of breath when he reached his destination: the heavy security door with the large number eight stenciled on it, eight long flights of stairs up the fire stairwell. He gripped the knob, and the door creaked open a crack.

He took a moment to get his bearings.

An overweight man stepped out of one of the inner offices. He was wearing a sweater, and his hair was slick with perspiration. Mattie smiled. *Finnerman. That has to be him.* Mattie watched the man leave his office, walk over to a coffee machine, and pour some coffee into a mug. The coffee spilled over the edge of the mug and down Finnerman's fingers. *Great. Byte's phone call must have really shaken the man.*

The next problem was getting past Finnerman's assistant.

He peered around the corner again and looked at the office area. The second office was Finnerman's, but the first office was unattended. Its door was closed, and the assistant's desk out front was unoccupied. Mattie lowered his head again and scooted over to the empty desk. He stayed low, away from Finnerman's view, and slid to the floor under the empty desk. Finnerman's office was now only a few feet away.

Mattie stopped to think. He needed a plan to draw Finnerman's assistant away from her desk.

Nearby, against the wall, was a massive Xerox copier working on what looked to be a big copying job. As Mattie watched, it churned out page after page, spitting sheets of paper into the collating shelves attached to its side. *Hmm.*

He crept to the copier, making sure Finnerman's assistant—who was faced away from him, focused on her computer—did not see him. He studied the collating shelves, and he was happy to see that they hung from the copier by a simple pair of hinge pins. *Good. This will be even easier than I thought.* He grasped the shelves and quickly lifted them away from the machine as a single unit. Now the copier, instead of stacking its copies in neat, collated groups, began firing sheets of paper across the office floor—at the rate of about two sheets per second.

Mattie slid back into his hiding place, quite pleased with himself, and waited until the assistant noticed the mess, gasped, and ran to stop the copier.

The moment she left her desk, Mattie scrambled toward the vice president's inner office. Luckily Finnerman himself was still standing at the coffee machine, sipping his coffee and staring at a spot near his feet, uncaring or unaware of the river of paper flowing across the carpet a few yards away. Mattie slipped into the office. He pulled Byte's note from his pocket, smoothed it out, and left it lying open on the desk.

Before Finnerman finished his coffee, and long before the annoyed assistant could clean up the flood of paper, Mattie slipped out of the office and made his way back toward the stairs. He stayed near the wall, his head low, moving swiftly away from the mess he had created. He found the door to the stairs, made his way down and out of the stairwell, and left the building through a side exit on the ground floor. A few moments later, when Finnerman found the note, no one would even know Mattie had been in the building.

He ran back across the street to the others, who were waiting for him with concerned looks on their faces.

"You were gone a long time," said Byte. "We were starting to worry."

"Did you do it?" asked Jake.

Mattie grinned. "As I said, piece of cake."

Finnerman sipped the last of his coffee and placed the mug back on the tray. *A million dollars!* he thought. *How am I supposed to get a million dollars by five o' clock?*

He returned to his office and closed the door. He was wondering how much the woman who had called him really knew. Did she really have proof against him? And who was she? Finnerman closed his eyes and let his head drop to the desk. Being an assistant to a master thief like Roarke was so *tiring.* He wasn't cut out for it. He closed his eyes, and they would have stayed closed except for the fact that he felt something tickling the end of his nose.

What the?...

It was a slip of paper with some writing on it. *Finnerman,* the note said, *here's proof that I am watching you. You cannot hide from me. You cannot escape. Have the million dollars by five o' clock, or my next phone call will be to the police.* The note was signed with a strange emblem of a circle crossing over a square.

Finnerman rose from his desk, and his legs wobbled beneath him. He stumbled to the door and peered around the eighth-floor lobby.

There was nothing to see.

His fingers trembled. Panicked, he returned to his desk and looked around his office. That picture on the wall—could a camera be hidden behind it? Was a microphone hidden in the potted fern? Finnerman stared around the room. Anything might hide a camera or a listening device. Perhaps someone he knew and trusted had learned his secret. Finnerman's mouth drew into a tight line. *No*, he thought, *this was not the work of a single person acting alone. Someone was able to get past the front desk and the security guards—even past* me—*without anybody seeing him—or her. There must be a whole team of them, a team of professionals.*

He gulped and realized what he had to do. He had to escape. He had to get to Roarke. Roarke could protect him. After all, Roarke was used to being pursued by people. He spent his life running away from the police.

Finnerman, struggling to breathe normally, grabbed his travel bag from behind his desk. Thank goodness he had brought it with him.

With his bag in hand, Finnerman scurried from the office. His assistant, who was still on her knees amid stacks of uncollated copies, stared at him in surprise as he ran toward the elevator.

"Mr. Finnerman," she asked, "are you leaving? What about the Radcliffe account?"

"Take care of it," he growled, and the elevator doors closed after him.

"Bingo," said Peter. "He's leaving. Let's roll."

The four of them were in Jake's old, sky blue Ford Escort. Finnerman, driving a silver Volvo sedan, pulled out onto the road and headed toward the freeway. Jake followed at a distance, staying just close enough to keep Finnerman's car in sight. Mattie, who was sitting in the back, leaned forward and pointed over Jake's shoulder. "Hey," he said, "Finnerman's taking the Old Shore Road cutoff."

He was right. The Volvo veered onto the entrance of Old Shore Road. Jake changed lanes to follow him, and he slowed down to increase the distance between the two cars. "Not much traffic on Old Shore Road," he explained. "I don't want him to see us."

The two cars began the winding journey up the edge of the cliff. As before, the shore of Bugle Bay spread out below them, and Peter could not help thinking how much more beautiful it seemed when he wasn't in danger of falling into it.

The trip took nearly forty minutes. Finnerman, driving erratically, zipped past the road to Mattie's house, past the road to Peter's house, and headed into the open country. When the road leveled and became safer, he increased his speed, and Jake sped up to follow.

Eventually the road curved behind some trees, and on the right a tall brick wall rose around the far end of the bend. A forest of pines rose up from behind the wall. Up ahead, the Volvo slowed and passed through the gate in the brick wall.

"The wall goes on for a couple hundred yards," said Jake. "That must be one huge house back there."

"It would be a pretty cool hideout," said Mattie.

Jake pulled off the road and the four of them got out of the car. The gate was just ahead, and they walked toward it carefully in case a security guard was posted there.

"For now," said Peter, "let's just take a quick look around."

When they were sure no guard was there they crept to the wrought-iron gate and found it closed. Peering through the bars, they saw a tree-lined cobblestone drive wind for perhaps a hundred yards toward a dark brick mansion. The heavy growth of trees cast long shadows across the mansion. Sunlight filtered through the leaves, creating deep, eerie shadows.

"We're not going up there, are we?" asked Mattie. The tone of his voice made it clear to Peter that he, too, had noticed the mansion's foreboding appearance.

"No," he whispered. "Not yet."

He raised the binoculars and was suddenly very grateful that Mattie had brought them. Peter was quite content to take a look around without having to get any closer to the house far down the road. He trained the binoculars on a large picture window and adjusted the focus.

"There he is!" Peter said. "He's talking to somebody, and he looks pretty excited. His arms are motioning all over the place."

Finnerman was pacing back and forth in front of the window, and his arms were indeed gesticulating wildly. Another figure joined him, and Peter shifted his attention to this newcomer. At first, Peter saw nothing but a mass of wavy silver hair, but then the features of the man became clearer. He saw the sharp nose and high forehead of a man whose face he had seen before. He gasped and dropped the binoculars, letting them dangle from his neck by their leather strap. "Malcolm Roarke," he whispered.

"Who?" asked Jake.

"Someone my dad's been after for a long time," Peter said. "He's real trouble. If Finnerman's mixed up with this guy—wait a minute!"

Even from this distance, Peter could see a third man moving near the window. He grabbed the binoculars to get a closer look. The man was tall, at least a head taller than Roarke, but he was also thin and had sharp, bony features. Worse, there seemed to be an emptiness in the man's expression. Peter wondered if the man had ever harbored a loving thought.

"We must be crazy," murmured Peter under his breath.

He lowered the binoculars, but his eyes remained fixed on the figure in the window. Peter was almost hypnotized by the newcomer's pale skin and deep-set, shaded eyes.

"Hey, Peter," said Byte, "are you okay?"

"Yeah," said Peter. "Sure. I'm fine."

Mattie moved closer and tried to see what Peter was staring at. "What do we do now?" he asked.

Peter frowned. *Roarke's involved. Finnerman's working with him.* The conclusion was obvious and frustrating: *the two of them have the chip.* But Peter had absolutely no way to *prove* it.

"There's still time before dark," Peter said. "We'll try to reach my dad and Lieutenant Decker right away."

"What if we *can't* reach them?" asked Jake.

Peter calculated the possibilities as though they were a series of chess moves. Roarke and Finnerman would not hold on to the chip forever. They would have to sell it— and soon. Maybe they would even leave tonight. Once they did, the law would never catch them. Peter thought of Mattie's proud grandfather humbled by false accusations. He thought of the car chase and how he and Jake had almost been killed, of his treasured car resting crumpled in a garage. He would not allow Roarke to escape.

"In that case," he said, "we'll come back ourselves."

ool!" shouted Roarke. "You simpering idiot!"
Finnerman was cowering, tears streaming down his
face and dropping onto his collar. He had been blabber-
ing some ridiculous story about blackmail, and Roarke
had long since worn out his limited patience. "All right,
Finnerman," he said. "Last chance. Slow down, take a
deep breath, and tell me again what nonsense has
brought you to me after I specifically told you *never* to
come here again."

Finnerman blubbered for another moment, then
finally gathered himself together. He wiped his nose,
stared nervously at Krohg, and tried to repeat his story.
"They called my office and said they had proof I helped
steal the chip," he said. "They want a million dollars."

Roarke raised an eyebrow. "Proof?" he snorted. "What
nonsense."

"It's true," said Finnerman. "They knew about the chip. They threatened to turn me in." He fished around in his pocket and pulled out a tiny, crumpled note. "Look! See? I found this right on my desk. These are professionals, Roarke, I'm telling you. They got past all the security at InterTel, even past me."

Roarke studied the slip of paper.

The handwriting on the note was a bit scraggly, as though it had been written in haste. *And yet,* Roarke decided, *there is something distinctly feminine about it. It was no doubt written by the same woman who called Finnerman. And there is something else—something almost adolescent in the swirling, practiced loops of the handwriting.*

"See?" said Finnerman. "I told you. Professionals, right?"

Roarke feigned worry. "You're absolutely correct," he said. "In truth, Finnerman, your office was invaded by a band of elite professionals *who happen to be sixteen years old and attend the local high school!*" He threw the paper in Finnerman's face. Finnerman winced. "Idiot!" Roarke walked over to the window and stared out at the thick forest that surrounded the mansion. "It's not a group of professional thieves," he said. "It's not blackmail. It's *them,* those bratty teenagers. This 'blackmail' is nothing but a ruse to trick you into leading them to me."

Finnerman's face went ashen. "What are you going to do?"

"To you?" asked Roarke. "Or to them?" His voice took on a warm, almost fatherly tone. "Why, I have no reason to punish you, Finnerman. You've done me a favor. But those teenagers won't be able to resist sticking their noses around here. We'll be ready, and I'll deal with them as you should have."

Finnerman gulped. "I should warn you, Malcolm," he said. "One kid—Braddock? He said his father is an FBI agent."

"What? FBI?…" Roarke spun around and looked at Finnerman, wondering if it were another paranoid flight of fancy from that idiot's weak mind, or if it were possible.…Roarke was silent for a moment as something in his memory clicked.

"Braddock," he whispered. "Of course. Braddock lives in Bugle Point. How stupid of me not to have seen it sooner. Like father, like son." He looked over at Krohg, and a warm smile spread across his face. "Well," he said, "this will be a bit of a reunion, then, won't it? Remember Mr. Braddock, Mr. Krohg? The merry chase we had in Washington, D.C., a few years ago? Well, his son and some friends fancy themselves detectives. They are soon coming to visit us."

Krohg's voice was a low hiss. "And what if the FBI shows up?"

Roarke waved the question away. "These are children. They think they're playing a game. Grownups are not invited." He stepped over to a keypad on the wall and began punching in codes. The images on the security system screens flickered and changed with every touch of a button.

"Let us prepare for the arrival of our guests," he said.

There were no streetlamps on Old Shore Road. When the sun went down, the road became very dark, and the only light at this late hour was the hazy glow of the moon. Jake approached the last turn before the mansion grounds and steered the car off the road.

"Turn off your headlights," Peter said. "We don't want them to see us."

Jake cut the lights and the car rolled to a stop. The four of them, dressed in black, got out and stood at the entrance to the mansion grounds. Peter noticed that he was shivering, which was strange; the June evening was quite warm.

The Misfits had returned here alone. Peter's father had been out of the office, wrapping up a case. Decker was "unavailable," and the officer on the phone was unwilling to interrupt the lieutenant. Peter had been torn. He could not allow Roarke to escape, but he didn't want to endanger his friends, either. It had taken them almost an hour to form a plan. But it was a workable plan—a *safe* plan.

"Are we ready?" he asked.

They hesitated a moment. Byte, Jake, and Mattie looked at each other, then at Peter, then at each other again.

"I'm a little nervous, I guess," said Mattie.

"There's nothing to be nervous about," replied Peter. "It's not like we're going to try to capture them or anything. We're just looking for evidence. We get near the windows, we look around, we listen, then we leave. It's as simple as that."

"What if they catch us?" asked Mattie.

"They won't catch us!" Peter took a deep breath, controlling himself so he wouldn't speak too loudly. "Look," he finally said, "we can quit now. We can all go home, tell the police what we've seen, Finnerman gets arrested for illegal possession of a library book, and Roarke skips town before my dad even knows he's here. Is that what we want?"

The others shook their heads.

"Or," Peter went on, "we can go in there, spend a few minutes looking around, and maybe get a clue as to where they've hidden the chip. Then we go back to town, tell Decker what we've found, tell the FBI where Roarke is, and these criminals go to jail. Best of all, Mattie's grandfather gets his good name back."

No one said anything. After a moment, Jake looked at Byte and Mattie and nodded his answer. "All right," he said. "I'm in."

Byte and Mattie took deep breaths and nodded as well. "Okay," they agreed, "us, too."

Peter smiled and held out his hand. They were making a promise to each other, and Peter wanted to give voice to that promise. "Misfits forever," he whispered. The others placed their hands on his in the darkness and whispered back: "Misfits forever."

The iron gate guarding the driveway squealed as Peter eased it open. He stepped inside, the others following close behind him, and he led them away from the cobblestone driveway and into the thick grove. *Best to stay far out of sight,* he thought. The pine branches above them captured the moonlight and cast gray shadows onto the ground.

Peter directed Jake to the front of the house, he and Byte moved to the sides, and Mattie headed around to the rear. The plan was simple. Each would find a window, listen carefully, peek through it if possible, wait, and hope to learn something of value to tell the police. In exactly thirty minutes, the four would meet again at the road and escape with any information they had gleaned. *Simple and safe,* thought Peter. *I've covered all the bases.*

He moved more deeply into the woods. A video camera, guided by tiny whirring motors, followed him as he passed.

Malcolm Roarke leaned back in his chair and pursed his lips. A dozen small monitors set in the wall in front of him flickered from one scene of the mansion's grounds to another. The largest screen showed Peter crouching behind a fallen tree trunk just to the south of the mansion.

Roarke touched a button, and his voice echoed in one of the other rooms. "Mr. Krohg," he said, "our guests have arrived. You may welcome them at your convenience."

Byte set her feet down gently, wincing when dried twigs crackled loudly beneath them. The silence here was so great that even the tiniest of sounds was magnified, and the snapping of twigs seemed to echo in the quiet of the woods. An owl's hoot vibrated in her bones.

I'm okay, Byte comforted herself, *Jake's behind me.* If she had been stuck in a situation that required quick thinking, she would rather be with Peter. But a very scary-looking guy was somewhere in that house, and when "big" and "scary" were the problem, there was no question—Byte would rather be close to Jake. Peter, Byte decided, was like a cat—all brains and calculation and curiosity. Jake was more like a St. Bernard dog, all calm and strength.

She stared ahead. The house was not too far away, she decided. She could just make out a pale square of light that seemed to grow more intense as she approached. *Good. A window.* All she had to do was step out of the forest, cross a short span of lawn, crouch in the darkness by the house, and take a peek through the glass. Simple. Byte was fairly certain she could do it quickly without being seen—so certain, in fact, that she did not notice the sound of a twig snapping a few feet behind her.

The forest ended, the trees grew more sparse, and Byte hid behind the last of them as she stared across the grass at the mansion. She looked for motion near the window, shadows crossing the glass, but she didn't see any. *More good luck.* She took a deep breath, lowered her head, and ran across the grass. When she reached the window, she dropped to a crouch and waited.

When she hit the ground, something heavy slapped against her thigh. Byte looked down and realized that she was still carrying her computer in its nylon bag. She carried it so often and was so used to its weight against her shoulder that she had not even thought to leave it in the car.

Byte found that her heart was beating wildly, but not from the effort of running. The window ledge was just above her head, and the safety of the forest was perhaps fifty feet behind her. From inside the house came the sound of footsteps, and there was some scuffling that might have been the movement of a chair across a hard-wood floor. Byte's heart pounded in her chest. She took a deep breath, swallowed the lump in her throat, and slowly raised her head. A holly bush gave her a little cover. She stared through its branches and pulled a small clump of it aside so she could see a little better.

A man with thick, silvery hair—the guy Peter called "Roarke"—was sitting in an antique wing chair. The room appeared to be a den or library. Shelves of books lined the walls, and music played from a small stereo. Roarke was flipping through the pages of a book and sipping some red wine. He placed the glass on an end table, closed the book, and Byte thought he might get up and leave the room.

She could not have been more wrong.

Roarke turned and looked directly at the window—directly at *Byte,* as though he had known all along that she had been hiding in his yard.

And his lips spread into a grin.

Byte's eyes flared open. All sense left her, and she did exactly what her frightened mind told her to do. She sprinted toward the forest. They were *all* in danger. As soon as she was out of sight she would scream to the others to give up the plan.

The trees were just ahead. Byte was running so fast, and her mind was so filled with the terrifying image of Roarke grinning at her that she never even saw the shadow that suddenly loomed in her path. A figure stepped out of the darkness. A man's arm circled her waist and drove the breath from her. Long, spidery fingers clamped across her mouth. She was trapped. The man pulled Byte against him and spoke to her in a husky voice.

"Hello, little one," he said. "No need to struggle. I won't hurt you yet. But you will not scream—understand? Or I will ignore my orders and snap your neck like a matchstick."

Without another word, he lifted Byte off her feet and carried her, kicking and muzzled, into the house.

Jake crouched behind a marble fountain that decorated the mansion's front yard. An owl flew near, hooting as it passed. If it had remained silent, Jake might have heard a brief scuffling in the forest ahead of him.

He turned his attention to the house and reminded himself to be patient. He could have already made his way to a window, but he wanted to give the others time to arrive safely at their assigned posts. To bide the time, he stared up at the moon and at the blue glow it cast on the ground. He listened to the sounds made by insects. He crushed a clod of dirt under the heel of his shoe.

Finally he crept from behind the fountain and made his way past a rock garden toward the large bay window at the front of the house. He was right in front of the window.

He peered inside, but there was not much to see. One side of the room held a couch and coffee table; the other side offered a thick easy chair and a tall reading lamp. More interesting by far, Jake decided, was the series of television monitors built into the wall, stacked three sets high and four across. Even stranger, Jake thought, was the fact that the televisions were all tuned to the same broadcast. It appeared to be some kind of horror movie. There was a house with dark trees all around it, and Jake could just make out a lone figure crouching in the shadows.

And Jake noticed something else. The man on TV was wearing black pants and a dark shirt. *Come to think of it,* Jake thought, *his shirt is just like the one I'm wearing.* He

squinted and looked at the picture again just to be sure.
Yup, the guy on TV is wearing the exact same—

Jake began to realize what he was seeing. *Hey! That* is *me!* He raised his hand and made a slight motion with his fingers. The guy on TV did the same. *What am I doing on television?*

Before Jake could answer the question, a skeleton-like shadow rose behind the crouching boy in the television picture. The shadow raised its arm over its head, and Jake noticed then that a very similar, very real-looking shadow was just now falling across his left shoulder. He dove to the ground an instant before an arm swished through the air behind him. Jake, rolling, spun around and looked up to measure his attacker. Jake was not too worried by what he saw. The man looked to be about a head taller than Jake, but he was thin, almost sickly.

The moonlight flitted across the man's face, and the teen finally saw his attacker clearly. The man had pale skin, a long, narrow nose, and tiny black eyes set deeply above high cheekbones. He moved, Jake thought, like a giant insect.

And he was quick.

The man's arm swung again, and a rocklike fist struck Jake on the shoulder and sent him sprawling. He struggled to his feet, but his attacker came at him again, his arm raised like a club.

Jake was ready. He ducked and slipped behind his attacker. The man stumbled, not expecting Jake's quickness, and Jake grabbed him in a wrestling hold. For a moment his attacker seemed helpless. Then the man made an odd twisting motion, a martial arts maneuver, and Jake's hold came undone like a loose shoelace. The man held Jake's hands in his, with his pinkies extended as though he were holding a pair of porcelain teacups. His thumbs pressed into the nerve clusters in Jake's palms, and pain shot up Jake's arms to his shoulders, dropping him to one knee. Before Jake could recover, the man spun into a kick that hit Jake in the chest and sent him crashing into the rock garden.

Jake stumbled to his feet. He had bitten his tongue when he fell, but the pain just made him angrier and more focused. The man came toward him, looming above him, looking more and more like he had crawled out from a grave. Everything seemed to be moving in slow motion. Jake, waiting for the right moment, balanced his weight on the balls of his feet and tightened his right hand into a fist. When the man was close enough, Jake shot his fist forward like a cannonball. A quick, slight shifting of his weight would drive it right into the face of his attacker. The man would drop to the ground, and Jake would call to the others.

Jake struck his attacker hard, his fist thudding into the man's face. But it was like punching a bag of cement mix. The man's head barely moved with the blow. Jake stared at his own limp, aching hand.

The man's lips, cut and swelling, twisted into a smile. He grabbed Jake in a headlock. Jake struggled, but the man had too much of an advantage. The front door of the house opened, and like a huge mouth, it swallowed up Jake in its darkness.

Peter did not hear Jake's struggle, nor did he hear the sound of the front door opening and closing. His mind focused instead on the ground in front of him. There in the dirt, pressed like smudges on a glass tabletop, were several tracks of footprints. The prints were fresh, perhaps only a few hours old, for Peter saw no evidence that wind or rain had disturbed them. *Interesting,* he thought. *What's so important out here, Mr. Roarke, that you spent your afternoon walking around in the dirt, hmm?* Several possible answers occurred to Peter: Roarke had buried the chip in the garden to hide it until he could escape, Roarke had explored the garden to see how hard it was for someone to approach the house without being seen, or…Roarke had set a trap for anyone who might arrive here.

Peter's eyes scanned the garden. He looked for trip wires hidden in the grass. He looked for searchlights mounted on the house. He listened for footsteps. But he found nothing. Nearby a video camera hummed, but Peter was too engrossed in his search for clues to hear it.

He made his way slowly to the window nearest him. He did not want to get too close, because he was afraid the light from the window would spill across his face and reveal his presence. Instead, he stood in the darkness

128 next to the window and listened. He could, in fact, hear a jumble of muffled conversation, but Peter was unable to grasp what was being said. He did not want to endanger himself by looking in the window, but it appeared he would soon have to do just that if he wanted to understand what was happening inside.

And there was something else....

A slight breeze brushed his hair against his face and carried an odd scent. *What is it?* He had been trying to concentrate on the voices, trying to gather clues, but this smell distracted him. *It's like an animal smell, a musky scent.*

Like one-hundred-dollar-an-ounce manly *musk.*

Peter hung his head. He knew he had lost this particular game of chess.

"Hello, Mr. Finnerman," he said. "How long have you been watching me?"

A clicking sound from behind him preceded the glare of a flashlight. Peter held up a hand to shield his eyes. Standing just a few feet away, hidden in the shadows, was Bill Finnerman. He leveled a gun at Peter's chest.

"How did you know I was here?"

Peter tapped the side of his nose. "You should try a better aftershave."

"You fell right into my trap," said Finnerman. He stepped out of the shadows and into the moonlight. Peter noticed he was smiling nervously, and perspiration was dripping from his forehead. The gun seemed very heavy in Finnerman's hand. "To the front door, please,"

Finnerman said. "I'm afraid you and your friends are going to be our guests for a while."

Peter shook his head. "You're not a killer, Mr. Finnerman," he insisted. "Let us go before you do something you really regret."

Finnerman's eyes dropped to the ground for an instant, and Peter watched his entire body sag. "I'm afraid it's a little too late for that," he whispered. His body stiffened, and his eyes, ghostlike in the pale light of the moon, rose to meet Peter's. Trembling, he cocked the gun. "No more discussion," he said. "Get in the house."

And so only Mattie remained outside the mansion. He made his way around the house. He had heard the *whirrr…click* of the cameras, and he had seen them watching him from the trees. It had actually been pretty easy to avoid them, once he realized they were there. The cameras could only cover so much area. Mattie, studying them, was able to move when the cameras turned away and hide when they turned back.

Now Mattie was crouching outside a window. He closed his eyes and, still breathing hard, wiped sweat from his face with his shirt sleeve.

He wasn't crazy about the idea, but he knew what he had to do next: He had to take a look through the window. It took Mattie a moment to gather enough courage, but when he finally peered over the window sill, his mouth went dry. On the floor of the room, looking every bit like a bouquet of wilting flowers, were Peter, Byte, and Jake. Standing near them were three men. One was Bill Finnerman, whom Mattie recognized from InterTel. The second was the guy with the wavy silver hair, the guy Peter called Malcolm Roarke.

And last, standing in the doorway with his arms crossed, was the third man. Mattie did not know his name, and he never wanted to get close enough to the man to learn it. The guy looked like a giant praying mantis.

Mattie ducked away from the window and crouched low in the dirt. *This is just great,* he thought. *Now what do I do?*

The night seemed to grow cold, and Mattie was alone with the darkness, the moan of the wind through the pines, and the rustle of dry leaves.

eter's eyes scanned the room.

Jake was glaring at Roarke. Peter thought Jake looked very much like a trapped bull contemplating a charge. Byte, at Peter's left, had drawn her knees up and wrapped her arms around them, resting her cheek against her shoulder. Pulled inward like that, she reminded Peter of a caged animal: fearful, but also watchful, angry, expectant.

What Peter failed to see was an avenue of escape. The obvious exit from the room was the door, and Roarke's henchman—the monster called Mr. Krohg—stood guarding the opening like some great, silent statue. The window was another option, but it appeared to be securely locked, and Peter did not relish the idea of diving through the glass. Besides, that sort of escape would involve abandoning his friends, and Peter's conscience would not even consider that.

"Well," said Malcolm Roarke, "what charming company. Since I will be your host for—well, let's just say *an undetermined length of time*—I should perhaps introduce myself to you children. I am—"

"—Malcolm Roarke," said Peter.

Roarke stared hard at Peter. One of his eyebrows arched for a moment, but then his face relaxed and he nodded. "Of course," he said. "The younger Braddock. I see you've inherited some of your father's formidable detective skills."

"I know about you," Peter went on. Peter figured if he could keep Roarke talking, he might gain the time he needed to come up with a plan of escape. "You call yourself Malcolm Roarke, but it's unlikely that's your real name."

Roarke snorted.

"—You've had several other names," Peter continued, "but those appear to be fake as well." He recited some of the facts from the file his father showed him: "You were arrested in 1985. The charges were dropped for lack of evidence. Arrested again in '95, same result. Since then you've spent most of your time in Europe. You've apparently acquired a great deal of money by stealing industrial secrets—like the 1286dx, for example—and selling them to the highest bidder."

Roarke's eyes widened for a moment, and Peter noticed a slight quiver in his upper lip. Once the man gathered his composure, however, his eyes narrowed to slits and his voice became low and gravelly.

"Impressive," he said. "Impressive indeed. But you are not the only one who has resources at his disposal." He grinned and stood over Peter. "Let me tell you what *I* have learned during my many dealings with your father....

"Your name is Peter James Braddock. You are sixteen years old, and you just completed your sophomore year at Bugle Point High School. You started school a year later than most of your comrades, and you skipped the fourth grade. When you were seven, your family doctor removed a mole from behind your left knee." Peter shuddered as Roarke continued. "Your father is FBI Agent Nicholas Aaron Braddock, a man with whom I have had dealings on more than one occasion, and your mother's name is Catherine. She organizes large business trade shows, which forces her to travel much of the time, and she sings with the church choir. How sweet."

Peter swallowed. The fact that Roarke had gone to great lengths to learn about the family of his enemy, Nick Braddock, made a chill run up Peter's spine.

"So you see," said Roarke, "I, too, make it a point to study my enemies."

Peter gazed at Roarke through the clump of hair that fell across his eyes. "What are you going to do with us?" he asked.

Roarke ignored the question. He strode over to where Krohg and Bill Finnerman were standing and began issuing his orders. "Escort them to separate rooms.

They're too mischievous together. Lock them in, and whatever you do, make certain you've removed anything from the rooms that might help them escape."

When Finnerman spoke, he made an audible choking sound. "Roarke," he said, "um, maybe we could just let the kids go. We could disable their car and be out of here before they could even walk home."

Roarke glared at him. "Don't be stupid, Finnerman," he said. "These 'kids' have already made a fool of you several times over. You've endangered the plan enough with your cowardice. I won't have you spoiling it further." Roarke's facial muscles tightened, his features hardening like some ancient, brittle wood. "Now," he said. "Start with the girl."

Finnerman looked at Roarke, then his eyes dropped to the floor. He walked over to Byte and took her hand. "You'd better get up," he said. "I'll escort you to a room."

Roarke sneered. "You're not taking her to the prom, Finnerman."

Byte rose and threw a glance toward Peter. She was asking for guidance. Peter's mind raced, and he closed his eyes when he realized he did not have an answer for her. He always seemed to have a solution for every problem, a plan for every moment, but here and now—when his closest friends needed him more than ever—he failed them. When he opened his eyes, he saw Byte throwing him a wide-eyed look over her shoulder as Finnerman led her away.

Krohg strode over to Jake. His deep-set eyes were tiny black dots, and his mouth opened to reveal large, gray teeth. "Get up," he said. He grabbed Jake by the collar and hauled him to his feet. The man's eyes glinted as though he were inviting Jake to throw another punch at him.

Jake shook loose from Krohg's grip and adjusted his shirt. He, like Byte, threw a glance in Peter's direction, but it seemed to say, *I'm all right, I can take care of myself.* Peter almost smiled. His heart ached as the sound of Jake's footsteps faded down the hallway.

At least, Peter thought, *Mattie is still out there. I hope he sees us and goes to get help.*

"Well," said Roarke, "here we are. Two leaders, eh? Come this way, Peter. I have something to show you."

Peter rose, and Roarke gestured him down the hallway to a large den or library. Bookshelves lined the walls, and many of the volumes appeared to be old, even hundreds of years old. A musty smell hung in the air. In one corner of the room was an antique wing chair crafted of burgundy leather. A Persian rug covered the floor, and a gold-trimmed Tiffany stained-glass lamp hung from the ceiling. Large works of art lined each wall, and Peter noted that one of the pieces appeared to be a Van Gogh.

"That's an original," said Roarke. "It's from my personal collection."

Peter looked at him. "Very nice. Who did you steal it from?"

Roarke only smirked. Several well-padded trunks were strewn about the room. Roarke was readying to pack up his valuables for his departure, Peter realized. Looking for any excuse to gain time, Peter made a circle around the room and examined each piece of art, each rare bit of porcelain, and the antique rolltop desk, none of which was of any interest to him at the moment. His circuit of the room, however, gave him some time and an opportunity to search for a means of escape. Going through the main door was impossible. It was solid oak, and Roarke would undoubtedly lock it upon leaving. The somewhat smaller door on the opposite side of the room was a better bet. It appeared to be lighter, and though Peter had no way of knowing where it led, he knew that getting through it might be his only chance.

He was concentrating fully on his plans of escape, until he stepped closer to the desk and saw...a chessboard and pieces. A game appeared to be in progress. Peter walked over to it, and he noticed a keypad with an LCD readout connected to the chessboard. It was as though the board had a calculator attached to it.

"Recognize it, Peter?"

Peter nodded. "It's a computerized chess game. The squares on the chessboard are identified with numbers and letters—this square is A-1, this is A-2, and so on. The computer's opponent types his move on the keypad, and the computer flashes back its response."

Roarke nodded. He paused and then gestured Peter over to the board. "Do you play?" he asked.

Peter swallowed. "Some."

"Good," said Roarke. "Analyze this position for me. It's white's turn to move."

Peter studied the pieces for a moment. As he did so, a tingle of fear spread through his body, but he could not figure out where the immediate danger was. *What* is *Roarke planning?*

"The game has just begun," Peter said. "Each side has exchanged a minor piece, though white has the advantage of the bishop pair. Black has brought his king to safety by castling. I'd say the position was about equal."

"Do you know how to operate the computer?"

Peter nodded. He studied the position for a few moments, then punched in a move. The LCD readout flickered for just an instant, and the computer flashed back a move of its own.

"Good move," said Peter, adjusting the pieces on the board to match the computer's readout. "This computer must be an advanced model."

Roarke snorted. "The best," he said. He leaned an elbow against the desktop. "Well, you and your friends present quite a dilemma to me, Peter. On the one hand, you are an annoyance and I would just as soon shoot the three of you and rid myself of you right now."

Peter felt a muscle in his leg begin to quiver. He placed his hand on the desktop for support.

"On the other hand," Roarke continued, "while I am an artist when it comes to thievery, I have not often

138 indulged in murder. I'm a businessman. Murder is not very—cost-effective, let us say."

Peter's throat went dry. His next words were barely audible. "What are you telling me?"

"Just this," the man continued. "You and your friends have brought some confusion, though minor, to my plans. You have intruded here at my home, and you have…*bothered* me. Make no mistake: If you attempt to cause any more trouble, you will have taken the decision from my hands. I will have to kill you."

A telephone rested on a small table near the desk, and Roarke reached for it. He unplugged the wire from the back of the phone, then tucked the unit under his arm. "Wouldn't want you to get any ideas," he said. He walked to the door and pulled a key from his jacket pocket. "Feel free to finish the game, Peter. The computer is a master level player, so it should provide you with some strong competition. You won't be leaving for a while." Then Roarke closed the door behind him. Peter heard the sharp click of the lock snapping into place.

He turned and stared at the chessboard. A light on the keypad blinked, inviting Peter to make another move.

Jake felt a bony but powerful hand clamp down on his shoulder as Krohg guided him through the hallway. The hand felt like a cold piece of meat. *Do not think about running*, its grasp told him. *Do not think about fighting. I am in control. You will obey me.* Krohg opened a door and shoved Jake into a dark, musty bedroom. Jake stumbled. If not for his size and weight, he would have slid across the floor and into a wall.

"I'll be watching you," said Krohg. The man's face seemed to crack as he smiled. "Try to escape. I would *like* that."

With that threat hanging in the air, Krohg left the room. He paused outside the door—as though, Jake thought, the monster were trying to remember something he had forgotten. A moment later Jake heard the key rattling in the lock.

Jake found a light switch and flicked it on. A four-poster bed stood in a corner, a thick layer of dust coating the pillows and blankets. The room's large walk-in closet, its door ajar, was empty.

Try the door.

He went over to the door and gripped the knob. It was made of brass, and it felt solid and heavy to the touch. Worse, he knew he couldn't break down the door. It, too, was solid, and Jake figured he could throw his weight against it for hours without causing so much as a dent. He'd need tools to try to remove the lock or hinges. *The window?* Jake tapped on the glass. It was some kind of thick security glass, and the frame around it was nailed shut.

Jake sighed. It appeared he would be staying here for a while. He sat on the floor, leaned his back against the bed frame, and told himself there was little he could do except wait and see what happened next.

140   He pulled his Superball from his pocket and bounced it off the wall.

"You and your friends should have stayed away," said Finnerman. "This whole thing could have passed without anyone getting hurt."

Except for Mattie's grandfather, thought Byte, but she couldn't quite bring herself to say the words aloud.

Finnerman led her to a room, a key sticking out from the lock on the door. He turned the key and swung the door wide. It creaked, and the noise reminded Byte of the sound of a coffin lid in old, phony vampire movies. Somehow a vampire seemed considerably less real and less frightening than the monsters living in *this* house.

Finnerman turned to leave and started to shut the door behind him, but he hesitated, looking at Byte. After a long pause, he whispered something that genuinely surprised her:

"I'm sorry."

Byte looked at him. "Then why are you doing this?"

Finnerman closed his eyes for a moment. The wrinkles around his eyes tightened into deep lines. He sighed, and then he pulled the door closed behind him.

The room was dark. Byte moved to a corner and slid to the floor. She did not pay any attention to the objects around her. She did not examine the room to see if she could escape. She merely wrapped her arms around her computer and clutched it to her chest.

The cameras were no longer a threat. Mattie had evaded them all, slipping from one tree to another. He was hiding now at the rear of the house. Just in front of him was a short concrete stairway leading down to a cellar door. Moonlight turned the door a pale gray-blue.

Far in the back, buried as it was, this underground entrance must have been easy to ignore. Its hinges were coated with a reddish-orange dust—where it seemed even the rust was growing rusty—and the base of the door was moist and streaked with moss. Over time, rainwater had backed up at the bottom of the steps and caused the wood to rot. The door smelled like a pile of old, wet leaves.

Mattie walked down the steps and gripped the knob. It made a quarter turn in his hand, but the door refused to open. The rusty workings of the lock caught and held. Mattie knew it would take someone a good deal larger and stronger than he to force the door open.

Then another thought occurred to him. *Maybe strength isn't the only answer.*

He stared at the door, at the way the water damage caused the lower panel to warp, and he wondered just how bad the damage was. He pried his toe into the mossy panel at the bottom; the wood gave and splintered. He bent down and tugged lightly at the panel, and a crack formed, tracing a jagged line halfway up the door. Mattie worked at the crack—gently, so he wouldn't make much noise—and a chunk of wood tore right off in his hand. The rotted piece very nearly crumbled in his fingers. With some probing, Mattie was able to make a hole large enough so he could reach through and unlock the door from the inside.

As he turned the knob once again and pushed, the door creaked open.

The cellar smelled the way Mattie imagined a swamp would smell—wet and warm and full of *things*. He moved farther into the darkness, and those smells were joined by another. It was familiar, but it took a moment before Mattie recognized it. *Metal,* he thought, *and oil. I'm around tools.* His fingers found a light switch, and he soon saw that the basement was a well-stocked work area: an electric drill and power saw, a series of wrenches and pliers, several different hammers, and dozens of screwdrivers.

Nearby, a machine came to life and started to hum. Mattie recognized the sound. It was the air conditioner, which pumped cool air into every room of the house. Mattie could see the unit just to his left, and he noticed as well the heavy, foil-coated piping that ran from the top of the machine to the air vents in the floor. Mattie felt a tingle along his spine. If he could pull one of those pipes down—and he was certain, with all these tools around, that he could—he might find a vent that led to a room where his friends were being held.

Then Mattie had another thought.

Just as many "bad guys" were in the house as "good guys." His chances of hitting the right vent, he guessed, were only about fifty-fifty. Suppose he pulled down one of those pipes and ended up staring nose to nose with Roarke—or his evil friend?

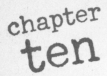

chapter
ten

Peter told himself not to panic. A thin sheen of perspiration covered his face as he circled the room, trying to remain calm, looking for a means of escape. It didn't help that his pulse was pounding fiercely in his temples.

The outer door is a lost cause. It might as well be made of steel and welded in place. The window, too, seemed impenetrable.

Peter forced himself to think. Roarke's offer to play chess had been tempting, for Peter loved the game and there seemed little else to do behind these locked doors. And yet, Peter somehow sensed that the offer was a lie, a trick. A chess game against this unusually strong computer was a waste of time, time he could obviously better spend working on a method of escape. Roarke wanted only to keep him quiet and occupied. Peter gazed at the game, then walked slowly toward the far wall.

The interior door. What was on the other side? Another room? A room with a window he could open? A room with a telephone? He might find nothing more than an empty closet or storage area, but then again, he might find something that would save all of them. Peter reached out his hand, which was still shaking, and grabbed the knob. It moved a little at his touch, but it refused to move any farther. Peter gave the knob a jiggle. If Roarke or Krohg were on the other side, he would have just given himself away, but he supposed a chance to escape was worth the risk.

Okay, then. Let's see how hard it will be to get through this thing.

He examined the door frame and the seam where the door and the frame met. There was a small gap there, no more than a sixteenth of an inch. Peter had heard his father talking about burglars who had broken through the lock of such a door with nothing more substantial than a credit card. They would insert the card between the lock and the door frame and jiggle it, and the door would often open.

Peter pulled out his wallet. He did not have a credit card, but there might be something…a photograph of Byte and Jake, a business card, his driver's license…. He needed something firm, something that would not bend so easily. Slips of paper, notes, a list of phone numbers, photographs—they all fluttered to the carpet from Peter's struggling fingers.

Then he saw it.

He smiled. It was perfect! He reached into the wallet and pulled out his B.P.H.S. student identification card. It was the right size, and it was laminated with a thick, plastic film. Peter slid it into the door frame, and he could feel it working against the tiny, spring-loaded bolt that kept the door from opening. The bolt shifted slightly, then clicked.

He gave the door a gentle push. It creaked, then opened an inch. Nothing but darkness was on the other side.

The hairs on the back of Peter's neck prickled. He was not afraid of the dark, but he was *very* much afraid of the sound he heard emanating from the other side of the door. It was quiet, so quiet Peter almost had to hold his breath to hear it, but it was definitely there. A barely audible hissing, the ragged *hsssss* of air passing in and out.

It was the sound of rapid breathing.

Peter tensed. He looked around for a weapon, and finding nothing suitable, he slipped off one of his Nikes and gripped it in his hand. If nothing else, he would give Krohg a big-time bloody nose if he had to. Sucking in a deep breath, Peter swung the door wide and leaped into the room screaming, with his Nike raised.

"*Yeeaaagh!*"

A shadowy figure bolted upright in the room, and Peter's leap caused him to land nose-to-nose with it. The figure screamed. Peter screamed back. The figure seemed to be about seven feet tall, though Peter wasn't really taking note of such details. All the yelling had startled him, and—because he had only one foot in a shoe and the other in a slightly worn sweat sock—his feet slipped out from under him. His rear end made a loud *whump!* when he landed on the carpet.

The seven-foot-tall figure leaned over him, and, in the light that spilled in from the other room, Peter could see that it wasn't a seven-foot-tall figure at all. It was a five-foot-tall figure holding a large brass lamp over her head.

Peter gulped. "Byte?"

"Peter?" Byte let the lamp drop from her fingers. It thudded against the carpet right next to Peter's head. "Omigosh...*Peter?* I'm so glad it's you. I thought it was one of them, and...."

Peter rose and rubbed the seat of his pants. Byte threw her arms around his neck and gave him a quick hug. "I'm glad you're okay," she told him. Peter's arms seemed like clumsy flippers as he returned the affection. *What is it about Byte that, even under these circumstances, makes me feel as though my brains are turning into oatmeal?* he wondered.

"I'm surprised all the noise we made hasn't brought them running," he managed to say. "They must be working in the far end of the mansion. Come on. Let's see if we can find the others and figure a way out of here." Peter and Byte moved back into the library. Once there, he grabbed the brass handle of the door that led into the hallway. "I can't see any way past this, though."

"The door on my side is the same," said Byte.

He tugged on the handle again, but the effort only made Peter more certain that the door was too heavy and too well made for them to get past. They sat down next to each other on the floor and rested their backs against the paneled wall.

Moments passed. Neither said a word. Peter, thoughtful, drew patterns on the carpet with his fingertip.

"I'm sorry I got you into this," he said. "We're in serious trouble, and it's all my fault."

Byte's nose scrunched up beneath the nose bridge of her glasses. "Your fault? Why?"

Peter shook his head. "I talked you all into coming here. I thought I could outsmart these criminals." He took in a deep breath and let it out very slowly. "I didn't even think of what would happen to us if my plan didn't work out. I've never had a plan not work out before."

Byte nodded as though she understood how he was feeling. Maybe, he thought, she agreed with him just a little bit.

"It's all right," she finally said. "I'm not blaming you." She angled her head down so that it was slightly touching Peter's shoulder. Peter liked the way her hair felt brushing against his upper arm.

"Say, Byte?" he said.

"Yeah?"

"Are you...I mean...is there anyone at school that you...you know, like or anything?"

Byte looked up at him. Peter realized she had very large, very pretty eyes.

"You mean...like as in *like?*" she asked.

Peter nodded. "As in...*really* like."

She didn't say anything. Peter saw a blush spread across her pale cheek. *Like a rose unfolding. Good,* he thought, ever the detective, *she's nervous. If she's nervous, it might be because it's* me *she likes.*

"Well...maybe," she said. "But I don't know if I want to say his name."

"Why not?"

Byte rolled her eyes. "It's *embarrassing.*"

They sat for a while in silence. Both remained quietly in thought until Byte, for some reason Peter could not see, perked her head up.

"What's that?" she asked.

Peter tried to follow her gaze. "What's what?"

"That," said Byte. "Over there. On the carpet."

She pointed, and Peter finally realized she was talking about a thin trail of wire that snaked across the carpet. "Oh, that," he said. "That's the wire to the telephone jack. Roarke unplugged the phone and took it with him. We can't call out."

Byte got up from the floor and picked up the end of the wire. She studied it for a moment, and then her face broke into a very large smile. The nylon computer bag was still slung across her shoulder, and she slipped it off now and held it out for Peter to see.

"Would it help," she asked, "if we could send a fax?"

Mattie felt his way along the cellar wall. The light he had flicked on didn't illuminate much more than the workbench, and he didn't dare stumble up the steps to the inside of the house to find the switch to light the rest of the cellar. He bumped his way past bags of cement and very nearly kicked over a large coffee can filled with rusty nails. His problem was not clumsiness. His eyes were following a trail of foil-covered tubing that led from the central air unit to a vent in the ceiling of the cellar. If only he could pick the right vent!

Most of the rooms above were silent. Mattie listened for the sound of footsteps, and occasionally he heard them, but they were far from the vents and they traveled for a long distance. *They must be walking down a long hallway.*

The foil tube led him to a corner of the cellar. He heard no footsteps, but a light, steady thumping came through the floor above him. Mattie could barely hear it: *Thump*…pause…*thump*…pause…like the beating of a heart—if the heart were made of rubber. Mattie smiled. He knew the sound. It was Jake, calming himself to the rhythm of his Superball.

Mattie reached up and tugged at the foil piping. It appeared to be no stronger than a padded envelope, so Mattie was surprised at how difficult it was to tear. He finally dug in his fingernails near the top and, holding his breath, pulled as hard as he could. The piping came away with a muffled tear.

He could see light through the vent. A moment later, the light was cut off when a large nose pressed against the metal grate.

"Hey, Jake," said Mattie. "What's new?"

Jake's mouth opened, then closed, then opened again like a fish's. "*Mattie?* How did you get down there?"

Mattie shrugged. "Just lucky. What's the situation?"

Jake took a deep breath. "I can't get out, and I don't know where the others are. The lock and the hinges on the door are real good ones, and the only way through either one is with a screwdriver."

Mattie grinned. "Cool. Regular or Phillips?"

"Are you almost finished?" Peter asked.

Byte stared at her computer screen, her face bathed in a blue glow. She was typing the last few words:

TO: FBI SPECIAL AGENT NICK BRADDOCK
FROM: PETER BRADDOCK AND FRIENDS

DAD,

WE'VE BEEN CAPTURED BY MALCOLM ROARKE. HE'S HOLDING US IN A MANSION AT 1510 N. SHORE ROAD. HE STOLE THE MISSING CHIP. 3 BAD GUYS. ARMED. SEND HELP. QUEEN'S GAMBIT ACCEPTED.

PETER

Peter looked over Byte's shoulder and nodded his approval. He only hoped his father understood the chess reference. He pulled his father's business card from his wallet and gave it to Byte. On the card was a telephone number for a fax line. "All right," he said. "Let's send it."

Byte plugged the phone line into the computer, typed in the fax number, moved the cursor to a button, and clicked the mouse: *Send Fax.* The machine whirred, and a message window came up moments later informing them that the fax had indeed arrived at its destination. Byte smiled.

"All done," she said. "What's next?"

"We wait," said Peter, and then he thought for a moment. Assuming his father was working late, which Nick Braddock frequently did, it was possible that he was reading the fax at this very moment. It would take a few minutes for him to notify the local police and organize a team, and perhaps another fifteen minutes before the team would arrive at the mansion. At that point, the situation at this old house was going to get mighty interesting.

Then his thoughts shifted.

He looked over at the computerized chess game. It was still waiting for him to move, its clock counting down the minutes before Peter would forfeit the game on time. Something he couldn't identify bothered him about the computer. Thoughts tugged at the edges of his mind, then danced away when he tried to grab hold of them.

"What are you thinking about?" asked Byte.

Peter's gaze didn't leave the pieces on the board. "I don't know why," he said, "but I'm thinking it might be a good idea to continue this chess game."

The lock on the door was set into a plate of polished brass. The plate itself was attached to the door with four screws. The screws resisted at first, but Jake merely gripped the tool more tightly and tried again. Each screw made a little noise—something like a cross between a pop and a creak—and then twirled out of the brass plate as though someone had just oiled it. *Okay,* Jake thought, *next step.* The plate came off with a gentle pull, and Jake stared at the inner workings of the lock.

Uh-oh. It was a little more complicated than he had guessed.

He began probing the lock with his fingers—tugging here and there and pushing at anything that seemed loose—and the center portion of the lock slipped right out. Another piece of the lock followed, and soon Jake had three or four pieces in his hand. The lock was coming apart like a Chinese puzzle.

Click!

The door opened.

Jake, quite happy with himself, was just about to break into a huge grin over his achievement when a hand clamped down on his shoulder and a voice spoke from behind him.

"Way to go, big guy."

The lock pieces flew from Jake's hand and scattered across the carpet like skittering bugs.

"Mattie!" hissed Jake, his tone a bit harsher than he intended. "Don't *ever* do that to me again! How the heck did you get in here, anyway?"

Mattie shrugged. "While you were working on the lock, I was checking out the rest of the cellar. Turns out a staircase down there leads right up into this room. The entrance is in the closet."

Jake looked past Mattie, and sure enough the closet door was open. He could see a small light on, and a wooden trapdoor stood on its hinges. "Sonuvagun," said Jake. "Well, come on. Help me gather up the pieces of the lock."

"Hey!" Mattie said, plucking a small brass piece from the floor. "The staircase to the cellar—we can use it to escape!"

Jake shook his head. "We have to rescue Peter and Byte first. And to do that," he added, "we need the keys. But don't worry, I have a plan."

No matter how hard Jake tried, the lock would not go back together.

"Here," said Mattie. "It goes like this." His fingers moved swiftly. In his hands, the collection of tiny pieces seemed to reassemble itself.

Jake tightened the last of the screws so he could feel as though he had done *something*. "There," he said, grinning. "I think we're ready for stage two."

When they were sure no one was in the hallway, Jake and Mattie stepped out and peered around them. Mattie had replaced the lock in its locked position. When the door clicked shut behind them, Jake noted with satisfaction that the lock held easily. No one—not Peter, not even Peter's *father*—would be able to tell from testing the door that someone had just escaped from the room. To his left the hallway stretched past perhaps a dozen large, closed doors, leading eventually to the open door at the end of the hall. Lights were on inside this last room. The boys heard a barely audible rumble of conversation.

"This way," Jake whispered.

To his right, the hallway made a sharp turn before ending at a smaller door. There was enough room in the alcove for one person, or maybe even two, to crouch out of sight. Jake pointed to the area, mouthing instructions all the while. *Hide there. Don't come out until I say. Follow my lead....*

Mattie hid, and Jake returned to the door he had just locked and pounded on it as hard as he could. He thought about yelling too, but he was afraid that his captors might be able to tell that the sound was coming from the wrong side of the door. He paused, banged again, then dove into the hiding place next to Mattie.

They waited quietly for perhaps forty seconds.

Jake heard the footfalls first. A shadow lumbered toward him, looming across the floor like a spreading oil slick. Then he heard the sound of Krohg approaching the door of the room where Jake had been held prisoner. A moment later, Jake saw Krohg lean over the lock and pull something from his pocket. Light glinted off metal. *Good,* Jake thought, *the keys. Now just go ahead and open that door, big guy, to see what it is I'm fussing about.*

The timing had to be perfect. Jake had to move right after Krohg opened the door, but before the man had the chance to remove the keys from the lock, so that Jake could lock Krohg inside. Jake crouched, muscles tensed. "When I come in there," Krohg grumbled toward the door, "I will break your arm. There will be no more pounding."

Krohg pushed the door open, and Jake took four steps to build up speed, then he lowered his shoulder and—*bam!*—struck Krohg right at the small of the back. Jake heard and felt a shallow *oomph!* as the air left Krohg's lungs. The force of Jake's tackle drove Krohg halfway across the room and headfirst into an antique vase, which cracked into several pieces and rained dried potting dirt onto Krohg's face. The brute stopped, shook his head, then turned and faced Jake, the makings of a dark bruise already spreading across his nose. His fingers squeezed into bony fists, then relaxed, as though he were preparing to wrap those fingers around Jake's throat.

Jake flinched and took a step backward into the hallway. Krohg growled angrily, and then, as though he had just realized what had happened, his eyes glazed over and went blank. Krohg tipped forward, landed in the carpet face first, and didn't move.

Jake looked in amazement at the brute lying on the floor. He had finally used his size and his strength to their fullest advantage.

So why didn't he feel good about it?

"What do we do now?" whispered Mattie.

Jake pulled the oak door shut and turned the key. "We find the others," he said, "and then we get out of here."

"You're really going to sit here and play chess?" whispered Byte.

Peter nodded. "Trust me," he said.

"Ohhh, right. Sure thing."

Peter moved, and the computer beeped its response almost instantly. Byte, curious, glanced over Peter's shoulder and frowned. "Hmmph," she said. "That's pretty fast. I've never known one of these things to calculate so quickly."

Peter shrugged. "Roarke said it was a master-level opponent."

Byte did not look convinced. "Still…."

Peter was not even sure why he was playing. Something—an instinct—told him to continue, and it made Peter more than a little uncomfortable. Roarke had had quite a gleam in his eye when he told Peter to play.

He concentrated on his next move, but his concentration was interrupted by a sound from the hallway. It was a jingling noise. A ring of keys.

Peter looked at Byte with alarm. "That has to be Roarke," he hissed, knowing that there was no time for Byte to run back to the other room. "Hide under the desk. We don't want him to know we've been talking."

Byte hid beneath the desk, and Peter waited for the door to open. He wasn't sure what he would say—something, he hoped, that would keep Roarke from entering the room.

The face that poked through the doorway was at least a foot lower than Peter expected it to be.

"Hi, Peter," whispered Mattie.

"*What?*"

Another face popped in. "Greetings, fearless leader," whispered Jake. "Ready to go home?"

Peter waved his friends into the room. He touched his finger to his lips to command silence. "How did you get the keys?" he demanded, his voice barely above a whisper. Four of them were in the room now, and greater numbers, Peter knew, meant a greater need for quiet.

"Long story," replied Jake. "Let's just say I made the team this time."

Peter nodded. He thought he understood. "Great," he said. "And I've got even better news. Byte and I sent a fax to my dad's office. The FBI is probably on its way right now."

Ten minutes ago

In the local office of the Federal Bureau of Investigation, a fax machine hummed. Special Agent Nick Braddock had gone out for a quick bite to eat before finishing a report. Special Agents Polaski, Billings, and Sandoval had joined him. Only Agent Clarence McNab remained, and Agent McNab was not too interested in the fax machine at the moment. He jabbed his plastic fork into a cardboard take-out container and speared another chunk of Kung Pao chicken, a spicy Chinese dish that he loved but the rest of the office hated—mainly because it often left Agent McNab with a nasty case of bad breath.

His time on the bureau obstacle course this afternoon was not what it should have been. Actually, it was horrendous. And his practice on the shooting range had not gone well either. There had been whispers in the office that maybe, just maybe, Clarence McNab was not quite FBI material.

I'll show them, he thought. *I'll show them I can be the best agent they ever had—that's what I'll do.* He wiped sauce from his face with a napkin.

The fax machine beeped as it finished printing. But, instead of grabbing the fax, McNab speared another chunk of chicken and washed it down with Diet 7-Up.

The fax would probably just mean more paperwork to fill out anyway, he told himself. It could wait.

chapter eleven

ill Finnerman ran into the room where his empty duffel bag lay. He shut the door behind him and let his weight sag against it. *Think,* he told himself, *breathe.* Things were moving so fast. *We will be leaving tonight,* Roarke had said. *A change in plans.... The presence of the kids has altered everything.... A week's worth of preparations in only a few hours....* Roarke had spoken these words coolly, for he was nothing if not cool, but Finnerman had seen the chipped-ice look in Roarke's eyes; he had seen the man's lips go pale and turn to thin white lines. Roarke did not like it when he had to change his plans.

And so a few minutes ago he had handed Finnerman the package.

"You will use this when the time comes," he had said. "You will not hesitate."

Finnerman held the package in his hands and tried not to let his fingers tremble. It was a padded envelope. It was weighty in his palm, and he dreaded opening it, although that was the reason he had run here, pretending to pack hurriedly even though he knew they were not leaving for hours.

Finnerman sat down on the bed and stared at the envelope. He pulled at the flap a bit at a time, shredding off tiny pieces so his progress was comfortably slow. The staples popped, and the tiny hole he had made widened to a jagged mouth.

A moment later, the gun fell into his hand.

It was a Walther PPK, a German gun, .22 caliber. Small enough to hide in a jacket pocket. Finnerman remembered that James Bond carried one in the movies. He hated it. He had never even held a weapon before tonight, let alone fired one. It felt cold, heavy in his hand, and it smelled of oil. It was so black that it was blue—like Superman's hair in the comic books Finnerman had read as a child. He held the gun in his palm and imagined firing it. The noise, even in his mind, was painfully loud. There was smoke, a spurt of flame from the barrel, and the smell of burnt powder, not to mention a wounded person, if his shot hit the mark....

He thought of the teenagers locked in rooms on the other side of the mansion. They would be the gun's next victims. Roarke had given him the gun because the job of killing the kids would be *his* job. It was a test. Finnerman had to prove his—what? His courage? His loyalty? No, it was something more. Roarke wanted

Finnerman to ante up. Finnerman's chips had to fall with those of Roarke and Krohg; he had to join the game—completely. If Roarke or Krohg killed the kids, then Finnerman was an accomplice. If Finnerman killed them, he was a *partner*.

Finnerman fidgeted with the gun, his hands shaking. His fingerprints would be on the gun—were *already* on the gun—and Roarke would see that they remained there. He would own Finnerman forever. The gun would disappear after the murders, but it would always be Roarke's to find. "Finnerman," he would say, "remember that incident with the teenagers? Well, I need you to do another favor for me…" And it would never end.

Finnerman, because he did not know what else to do, grabbed his bag, went to the dresser, and pulled open a drawer. He tossed in a few pieces of loose clothing. And the gun. The clothes dribbled over the edge of his bag, and he stuffed them in, not caring that they would wrinkle. He shoved in his shaving cream, accidentally spraying some into his palm. *Toothbrush, aftershave….* He worked faster, barely noticing the sweat that streamed down his cheeks until some of it got into his eyes and made them burn.

The faster he worked, the easier it was to forget about…about….

He lifted the bag, still very much in a hurry, and its weight suddenly shifted. A dirty sock and some lime green boxer shorts fell out, and a solid object—the gun—landed on top of them.

And there, lying wrinkled among the clothes, was the photograph. His Cub Scout picture. Finnerman had forgotten about it. He lifted it now and stared at the little boy he once was—the little boy who was too fat, who lived through stories in books and movies, and who never had a friend. A misfit with merit badges. Finnerman studied that picture and wondered where that little boy had gone.

Silly question.

The fat little boy had grown into a fat adult who was sitting alone in a room contemplating the murder of three innocent teenagers. Finnerman slumped to the floor and covered his eyes with his hands. It was as if the photograph had punctured him. All the lies he had been telling himself about the money and the life of leisure in exotic places spilled out of him like water from a sieve. The boy in the picture seemed to be asking: *Is this the life you're offering me?*

Finnerman didn't like the future he was facing.

So then, he thought, he would have to change the circumstances. If he wanted a different future, he would have to start planning it now. Finnerman wasn't sure he could do it, wasn't sure he had the strength.

But the little boy in the picture was asking him to try.

In the FBI office it was that sleepy time late in the evening when only a few agents remained and the quiet of night was settling in. Agent McNab was holding on to his somewhat expanded belly and trying his darnedest not to let any of the other agents hear him groan. Agent Polaski was cleaning his gun. He was *always* cleaning his gun, McNab thought. Who was he trying to impress? Agent Sandoval signed the last of a thick stack of papers and walked them over to a file cabinet.

Nick Braddock finished printing out the last page of his report and dashed off a signature. No one would be able to read his name, but he was anxious to get home, and the bureau didn't grade penmanship. He walked his report over to the bureau chief's office and left it on the desk. The boss wanted to see it first thing in the morning, so Nick would make sure it got on his desk tonight. Besides—

Hmph. A sheet of paper was lying in the fax machine.

"Hey, McNab," called Mr. Braddock, "what's the incoming fax?"

McNab looked up and shrugged. "Dunno."

Nick took the fax and read it. For a moment he did not react at all, but then the muscles in his jaw tightened, and his eyes narrowed to a squint.

"What's up, Nick?" asked Agent Polaski.

"McNab!" Nick shouted. "What do you think you're *doing?* This fax has been here for 45 minutes!"

Agent McNab's eyes widened in realization and fear. Had he messed up again?

Nick Braddock hurriedly read the note again. It did sound like Peter, and it was just the sort of trouble he'd get mixed up in. "Queen's Gambit Accepted." The chess reference was Peter's way of proving he had written the note, but it also meant something else: Peter was losing this game to Roarke. Peter had taken a risk, and Roarke had capitalized on the mistake. Peter had blindly taken the offered pawn.

Nick Braddock began barking orders. "Polaski, call the Bugle Point PD," he said, "and tell them we have a hostage situation at 1510 North Shore Road. Inform them that the FBI will be handling the case, but that we request immediate backup from their SWAT team. Tell 'em we've got three armed perps and four hostages. McNab, you'll partner with me. Polaski, you and Sandoval will handle the air support. I want a chopper fueled and ready in ten minutes."

"All right," Peter said, "here's the plan."

The four crouched on the floor of the library. Jake was smiling slightly, and Peter understood why. For the first time since entering the house, they were on the offensive. "We'll go through that door and into the next room," Peter went on. "We'll try the key from in there. The less time we spend in the hallway, the better." He looked at the others. "After we get out of that room, we'll make our way down the hallway toward the rear of the house. It's a shame we can't escape through the trap door, but Krohg is locked in that room. Roarke and his buddies will see us on the cameras when we're outside, but I'm counting on the fact that we can outrun them."

Peter pursed his lips. He did not feel that the plan was well thought out. Still, it was the best and only plan he had. "Okay, then," he said. "Let's move."

The hallway itself was wide as well as long, designed to give the impression of spaciousness in a house that was absolutely enormous anyway. Antique brass light fixtures spaced evenly on the walls cast an eerie yellow glow.

Jake took the lead. It was a dangerous position, but if this final battle happened to get physical, Peter wanted someone with Jake's size and speed in front. He felt awful about placing his friend in danger, but Peter knew the others were counting on him to make such choices. Just ahead the hallway made another break to the left, and he signaled Jake to take the turn.

They found themselves at the entrance to the kitchen. Like the other rooms in the house, this one seemed more like a vast cave than like a room in someone's home. They crept through the door and into the darkness, and Mattie slapped his hand over his mouth when he stubbed his toe against the bottom edge of an island stove. Above them, copper pots hung from a wooden beam. Jake's forehead whacked into one, and the pot began to sway. It gave out a rusty creak, and it cast a black, swinging shadow against the moonlit wall.

Yes, thought Peter, *this is where we want to be. The dining room must be very close.*

He was right. Swinging oak doors led them into a room with a parquet floor and an ancient, worn banquet table. Peter's hopes rose when he saw exactly what he had expected to see at the far end of the room: A set of French doors. They were bordered with fine draperies and overlooked a flagstone patio. Peter pointed so his friends could see. *An outside door,* he mouthed as they all moved toward it. *We'll leave that way.*

Jake reached for the door and tugged. It wouldn't budge, and they heard something jangling on the other side of the glass. They all stared. It was a chain, and dangling from the chain was a heavy lock. A chill crawled up Peter's spine.

Peter's instinct to break the glass came a moment too late. The room flooded with light.

Peter and his friends pivoted, and in the doorway was Malcolm Roarke. A chrome-plated .45 with a laser sight was in his hand. Krohg stood next to him, holding a rag filled with ice against the angry blue-black bruise that spread across his nose and cheekbones.

The barrel of the gun rose and pointed at Peter first.

"Step away from the door, please," said Roarke. "I'm afraid you've quite tried my patience. Move back to the library. *Now.*"

The gun was very persuading. Peter and his friends moved away from the door, and Krohg strode ahead of them. Roarke remained in the rear. Peter felt the barrel of the gun pressing into his spine as he trudged back down the hallway and into the library.

Roarke looked at Mattie. "I'm so glad that the fourth member of your little group is able to join us. Line them up against that wall, Mr. Krohg."

Peter flinched slightly as Krohg grabbed his shoulders and shoved him against the wall. Jake came next, then Byte, then Mattie. The four were lined up like balloons at a carnival shooting range.

Roarke pulled back the slide on the gun and chambered a bullet. "Young Mr. Braddock will be the last to go," he said. "He will have the honor of watching his friends die. That should teach him a lesson, though perhaps a little late."

Peter scanned the room: Krohg was guarding the door. Roarke had the gun. He could see no escape.

"We'll begin with the girl," said Roarke.

He raised the gun and pointed it at Byte. The laser sighting device cast a shimmering red dot of light that flickered on Byte's forehead, just above the nose bridge of her glasses. The creases on Roarke's index finger deepened as the man applied pressure to the trigger.

"*Wait!*" shouted Peter.

He looked at his three friends, at Krohg, at Roarke. He had yelled out in the hope that Roarke would stop, but now that Roarke had, Peter wasn't quite sure of what else to say. He stood silently for a moment, his tongue dry and thick.

And then an idea came to him.

Roarke turned the gun and pointed it in Peter's direction. Peter imagined that he could feel the point of red light burning against his skin. "What is it?" Roarke grumbled.

"I—I'm surprised at you, Mr. Roarke," Peter said. "When I saw the things you surrounded yourself with, I thought you had some class. I thought you were a man who appreciated the finer things in life." He pointed to the Van Gogh painting waiting to be packed away. "You gave me the impression you were a gentleman, a lover of fine art and classical music. I had no idea you were so—" Peter said the next word as though it were coated with vinegar, "*common.*"

Roarke bristled. "'Common'?"

"Why, yes. Only a common crook would use a gun and spill blood in a room filled with the finest in art and literature. Where's the art in blowing someone's head off?"

Roarke smirked. He waved the pistol nonchalantly. "I'm listening," he said. "Continue. What do you have in mind?"

Peter took a deep breath. The idea was taking shape. He just wasn't sure it would work. "Even a fox in a foxhunt has a sporting chance, Mr. Roarke. It isn't trapped in a barrel and a grenade tossed in. Let's make an agreement. A *gentlemen's* agreement."

"A wager, then?"

Peter smiled. "Yes. A wager." He gestured toward the chessboard and its still-blinking light. "Allow me to finish the game against the computer. If I lose, you…finish us off. But if I *win*," and here Peter looked at the others, "if I win, you let us all go, alive. Take the chip, grab a plane to whatever country you like, but leave us here—alive and uninjured."

Roarke chuckled and reset the safety on the .45. "You quite remind me of your father. I suppose I'm fated to deal with the both of you" He twirled the gun around his finger, caught it, and rubbed a loving finger down the length of its barrel to wipe off some perceived smudge. "A chess game for your lives, eh? How delightfully grotesque! Edgar Allen Poe himself could not have imagined better." He grinned. "Yes, Peter, I believe this idea of yours appeals to me a great deal." He took a few steps toward Peter, and his arm whipped around so that the barrel of the gun hovered an inch from Peter's nose. "You may proceed any time," he said. "Just remember: I'll be watching you. Tournament rules, yes?"

Peter nodded and swallowed. "Tournament rules." He walked toward the chessboard, and his steps carried him past his friends.

"Kick his butt," Jake whispered. "You can do it."

Peter shook his head. "Don't think so," he whispered back. "I'm just buying time."

He bent over and stared at the position. The game was worse than he had remembered. A quick look at the board told him that the computer had already captured one of his pieces, and his defensive outlook was weak.

Peter sat down at the desk and studied the board. He made a move, and with speed that made Peter blink, the machine flashed back its reply. Peter moved the pieces accordingly and studied the board again. He reminded himself he was playing not to win, but for *time*. Somewhere out there his father was looking for him. He only needed to make sure the game lasted long enough.

Roarke's voice came dripping up from behind him. "I know what you're thinking," he said. "Remember, we agreed on tournament rules, Peter. You'd better check your clock."

The clock! Peter had forgotten. Under tournament rules, each player has a given amount of time to make a certain number of moves, and the computer keeps track of the time each one spends thinking. If Peter took too much time, the computer opponent would automatically end the game and declare itself the victor. Peter and the computer had each started the game with sixty minutes of think time. Peter pressed a button to reveal the twin clocks. The computer's clock said ":14." In the ten or twelve moves they had played, the computer had used up only fourteen seconds of its allotted sixty minutes. Peter's clock said "52:18," and its numbers were clicking upward like the gauge on a gasoline pump.

"That's not fair!" shouted Peter.

Roarke looked at the computer readout and yawned. "Of course it's fair," he said. "You agreed to the game, Peter, and you agreed to play by the rules. It's not my fault you went off and left your clock running. You have seven and a half minutes to complete the game. Play on."

Seven and a half minutes! Since his plan to stall for time was thwarted, he had to try to win. He moved quickly, and the computer responded. Peter stared intently at the board, and the pieces came into sharp, clear focus as they did when he was playing his best game. They became larger and seemed almost to float above the chessboard. They were living things, soldiers at his command. He ordered them to form a protective barrier near his king, and the pieces responded. He offered them to the enemy army judiciously, trading away one of his pieces for another of equal or greater value. His loose position began to tighten.

But less than four minutes remained on Peter's clock.

The computer moved a pawn onto an unprotected square, and Peter sent his bishop careening across the board to snap up the hapless piece. He almost had time to smile before the computer beeped back its next move.

Only then did Peter realize his mistake.

The pawn had been a "poison pawn," a sacrifice offered to lure Peter into a weaker position. The trick had worked. Peter stared at the board, ignoring the ticking clock as he tried to cobble together a new defense. He started to reach for a piece, but he knew it was hopeless. Only thirty seconds remained. Instead of playing a move, he looked over his shoulder at his friends and mouthed a simple, two-word apology.

I'm sorry.

Roarke cocked the pistol and placed it at Peter's temple. "Nothing personal, boy," he said. "It's just business."

For an instant it seemed that time stopped completely. The gun barrel froze at Peter's left ear. Krohg was standing near the door, an evil grin on his face. A bead of sweat ran down Jake's neck as he scowled at Roarke. Byte held her breath as she stared at the gun. Mattie looked first at the gun and then, it seemed to Peter, in slow motion shifted his eyes to Peter's. Peter's breathing sounded loud and strained to him, like a rusty saw on wood. The stillness of the moment was broken by two sounds. Peter noticed first the distant, steady *thwup thwup* of a helicopter. The second was a loud, booming voice behind them in the doorway.

"What's going on here?" it demanded.

Roarke turned toward the sound. Everyone else, startled out of their frozen thoughts, turned toward the sound.

It was Bill Finnerman.

Roarke jerked his head to face him. Peter saw the surprise on Roarke's face.

At that moment the timer beeped.

"Well, Finnerman," Roarke said, his voice unsteady for a moment, "welcome to the party. Young Peter here has just lost a wager, and I am about to collect the debt."

Finnerman, his back straight and his shoulders squared, strode across the room. He faced Roarke and snatched the gun from his fingers, placing it carefully on the desk. Roarke seemed puzzled—either by Finnerman's quickness or his nerve—and stood silent.

"We haven't time for this," Finnerman reasoned.

"These kids have been an unnecessary distraction." Peter thought he saw Finnerman's lips tremble, but the man did not back down. He stood tall, his chin thrust forward. The effect was impressive despite the perspiration dripping off the tip of Finnerman's nose.

Neither man seemed to have heard the helicopter. *They will in a moment, though,* Peter thought. The sound was growing louder. Peter allowed himself a quick glance at the window, and he thought he saw the tiniest flickering of blue lights in the distance, possibly even at the gates of the mansion's drive. *Police cars?*

"I know they've been a distraction, Finnerman," said Roarke, "and they've annoyed me for the last time." He picked up the gun. "Now, step out of the way."

Finnerman didn't move. The *thwup thwup* of the helicopter and the flashing of blue lights were undeniable now. Roarke raised the gun, but as the noise from outside finally sunk in, he craned his neck toward the window.

"Police? *How?...*" He slowly turned back toward Peter with a brief look of admiration. He did not yell; there was no panic in his eyes, only a resolve to complete what he had started. "Move, Finnerman, quickly," he said. "I'm going to kill them. All of them. And we'll be finished with this ludicrous mess." He raised the gun and pointed it once again at Peter.

Finnerman refused to move. "No," he said quietly. "It's over, Roarke."

Rustling sounds came from the woods outside, and

flashlight beams crisscrossed and passed over the windows. Roarke never lowered the gun, for he had seen the nearing lights. He merely clenched his jaw and squeezed the trigger. Peter heard the blast and saw a tongue of flame leap from the barrel of the gun.

"Gunshots from the house!" Nick Braddock shouted into his walkie-talkie. "Repeat, gunshots from the house. Secure the area now! Do not wait to set up the perimeter!" Several Bugle Point police officers rushed the front door.

Nick Braddock stayed at his post and prayed fervently that the bullet wasn't meant for his son.

For a split second Peter waited for something small and white-hot to crash into his chest, but the bullet never arrived. Instead, something large, a gray shadow, moved in front of him and blocked his view of the gun. In the next instant, the shadow's full weight slammed back against Peter and knocked him into the wall.

The shadow was Finnerman. He hung limply in Peter's arms, and a spot of red blossomed and grew across his chest.

Roarke threw down the gun and ran across the room. It seemed to Peter that he was running in slow motion, but his movements were filled with an eerie sort of grace. Peter watched him, the man's jacket billowing behind him. Roarke leaped through the window. Tinkling shards of glass fell gently, like snowflakes, to the floor. Peter, still holding Finnerman's limp body, thought they sounded like wind chimes.

Roarke rolled when he struck the ground, then began to run. He knew the grounds well and he kept the bluff to his right, heading for the eight-foot brick wall three hundred yards ahead and the road just on the other side. His feet pounded against the grass, and in seconds he had vanished into the forest behind the mansion. The forest was thick, and the only real approach to the mansion was from the front. He knew there would be a few scattered police officers in the woods, perhaps some FBI agents, but there would not be many. The authorities could not have prepared a complete plan under such short notice. Yes, there was a chance.

The thickness of the vegetation slowed him as he ran, and dry needles crackled and twigs snapped beneath his feet, but he continued to hurry.

From behind him, Roarke heard shouting. They were already in the house. He could hear the commotion as the officers moved from room to room. Good. The longer they remained in the house searching for him, the better his chances of getting away. Finnerman and Mr. Krohg were done for, but Malcolm Roarke would survive.

A moment later the wall loomed before him. He could hear the snapping of twigs behind him and the pounding of another pair of feet, but he wasn't worried. Even in the bright moonlight, the police would never find him. They would never even know for certain that Roarke had come this way. He grabbed the low branch of a tree near the wall and swung himself up. Several branches bent over the wall, and he would be able to crawl out along one of them and drop to safety. In a moment he would be free.

But just as his feet landed on the other side of the wall, he heard a loud click followed by a hum. A thousand-watt spotlight came to life and bathed Roarke in its glow. Another spotlight came on, and then another, and to those lights were added the headlights of a half dozen cars. Roarke shielded his eyes from the painful brightness. Shadows moved around him, the black silhouettes of men holding weapons. It was a small army of police and FBI agents. Each held a shotgun pointed in his direction. One of the shadows stepped forward into the light, and the shotgun in his hand lowered toward Roarke's chest. Roarke recognized the man immediately.

"You," he croaked. "Braddock."

Peter's father pumped the shotgun and smiled.

Lieutenant Marvin Decker burst into the library with his gun raised. His partner Sam ran in behind him, and

178 the two detectives swung their weapons before them, scanning the room. Decker could feel the perspiration running along the back of his neck, but his training kept him focused, calm, and alert. He instantly assessed the situation: The kids were there, safe, and a guy was lying on the floor, bleeding from his chest. Decker pressed a button on his walkie-talkie. "We're in," he barked. He took another look around the room. "The hostages are fine. The situation is secure. Repeat, situation is secure."

"Hey, Lieutenant," said one of the kids—the Braddock kid, Decker remembered. "We could use some help here."

Decker nodded and issued an order for an ambulance. He looked over each of the teenagers. They were all a bit dazed, and the little kid had tears streaming down his face, but it looked like no one was hurt but Finnerman.

A click and static came over the walkie-talkie, then "Lieutenant? This is Chang with SWAT."

Decker raised the set to his mouth. "Go, Chang."

"Lieutenant, we've got another one here, at the back door."

"Good. Take him to the gate," Decker ordered.

"Lieutenant," said Peter, "I need to see my father."

"Who's your father?" Decker grumbled. Decker liked to grumble, especially when things were going his way.

"He's one of the FBI agents outside."

The lieutenant nodded. "Okay," he said. "FBI's working their way to the back of the property. Seems like your other buddy ran into a group of them. You can go, but I need you back for your statement."

Decker holstered his gun. He reached into his coat pocket and removed his tin of aspirin. He flipped a tablet into the air and caught it in his mouth. Smiling, he offered the tin to Sam.

"Want one?" he asked.

Peter ran outside, loped to the driveway entrance, and broke into a dead sprint as he rounded the corner and headed toward the rear of the house. Some SWAT team officers were escorting a handcuffed Krohg toward the front gate. He glared as Peter ran by him. A helicopter circled above, its spotlight scanning the ground. Other lights shone in the street ahead, and police officers stood watch over a lone figure handcuffed and cringing against the brick wall. The figure was Malcolm Roarke. Nick Braddock stood a few feet away, speaking into his walkie-talkie and coordinating the final mop-up procedures.

"Dad!" shouted Peter. He ran over to his father and let Nick Braddock's strong arms encircle him.

"I was just thinking," whispered Nick Braddock, "that as much as you've been through tonight, it's nothing compared to what's going to happen to you when I get you home." He stepped back, his hands on Peter's shoulders. "Are you and your friends all right?"

Peter nodded. "Just fine." He pointed to Roarke, and he raised his voice so everyone could hear. "He stole the 1286dx computer chip," said Peter. "He kidnapped us, and he threatened to kill us."

Roarke looked up and chuckled. Peter shivered at the sound.

"Nonsense," said the villain. "I don't know what the boy is talking about. I know nothing about a computer chip. I was spending a quiet evening at home when this juvenile delinquent and his friends trespassed on my property. I placed him and his hoodlum accomplices under citizen's arrest until you arrived. Cuff the boy, officer. I wish to press charges."

"He stole the chip!" Peter insisted. "He's guilty!"

Roarke grinned. "And where is this chip, boy?" he asked. "Where is your proof?"

The police hesitated. They weren't about to let Roarke go, but his challenge certainly had to be answered.

"Peter," whispered Nick Braddock, "do you know where the chip is?"

Peter thought. As small as it was, the chip could be anywhere—in a teacup, in a matchbox, in Roarke's shoe. Peter certainly hadn't seen it lying around anywhere. Then he remembered something Byte had said earlier in passing. Now her words were like arrows pointing right at the missing computer ship. Peter nodded to himself. *Of course. That has to be it.*

"I think I know where it is," he announced. "We'll have to go back inside."

"I'm right behind you," said his father. He pressed his palm between Roarke's shoulder blades and gave the prisoner a shove. "You're coming too."

Peter led them back into the library. Jake, Byte, and Mattie were still there giving statements to Decker, but Finnerman was already gone, rushed in an ambulance to the hospital.

Peter circled the room and approached the massive antique desk in the corner. A heavy marble paperweight sat on the desk, and Peter lifted it, hefting it in his hand to test its weight.

"Is the chip hidden inside the paperweight?" asked his father.

Peter looked at Roarke. The man was smiling again. Peter's fingers tightened around the paperweight, and his other hand traced a pattern across the top of the computerized chess game. Peter felt for a warm spot along the keypad. When he found one, he yanked out the plug from the keypad's AC connection.

He took a deep breath, then in one swift motion, Peter brought the paperweight down with a crash. It landed on the game's playing area, scattering the pieces and cracking the hollow, plastic board. He saw nothing, but of course Peter had not expected to find anything *there*. He tugged at the broken plastic until he came to the wiring under the keypad. Now he had to be more careful. *The electronics,* he thought, and he smiled. *The computer did make its moves very quickly, didn't it, Byte?* He gently pried up the top until it snapped off in his hand, revealing the complex circuit boards and wiring underneath. Peter eased his hand inside the computer and tugged out an object that was no bigger than a nickel.

It was the 1286dx.

Peter held it up for everyone to see. Then he looked Roarke in the eye and said the only word that seemed appropriate.

"Checkmate."

epilogue

One week later

byte worked her way through the long line of people, watching for her friends in the crowd. She wasn't entirely sure why she was here. Jake had called her, and he had been terribly mysterious in his instructions. "Meet me at the Bugle Point Recreational Hall," he had told her. "Eight o' clock. Saturday. Don't be late." That was all. No explanation, no hints. Byte had pressed him, and all Jake would say was "Dress nicely."

She crinkled her nose beneath her glasses as she looked for him. *I hate secrets. Surprise parties, friends "kidnapping" you on your birthday—yuck! Surprises are only fun if you know about them in advance; otherwise, they're just embarrassing.*

Just then Byte felt a familiar tapping at her left shoulder. She turned, but no one was there. *Who else?* she thought. Knowing what would happen next, she slapped her hand down on her right shoulder just in time to trap someone's finger. She turned around.

Mattie was looking up at her, cradling a stack of small booklets in his free hand.

Byte sighed. "Hello, Mattie," she said, still gripping his finger.

Mattie grinned and tugged the finger away. "I couldn't fool you this time," he said. He took one of the booklets and handed it to Byte. "Here," he said, "have a program."

"Okay, but—"

Mattie moved back into the crowd and was gone. Byte threw up her hands, and because she had no idea what to do or where to go next, she took a moment to look at the program: "Summer Jazz Festival," it announced, "An Evening of Music Sponsored by the Bugle Point Recreation Department."

Jazz festival? Why had Jake invited her here?

Then something occurred to her. Was this a...*date?* She drew in a breath, and several seconds passed before she realized she had not released it. A date with Jake? Byte was afraid to believe it was true. When Peter had asked her who she liked, she had been too embarrassed to say. Even now, she was almost too embarrassed to admit it to herself. But the answer was...Jake. Byte looked around as though someone might have heard her thoughts. She rolled up the program in her fist, sure that the sudden warmth she felt meant that her face was turning red.

"You look very nice tonight," said a familiar voice.

Byte turned so quickly she had to catch her glasses. She was startled to see both Peter and his father standing there. Peter was wearing—*wow!*—a sport coat and tie, and the clump of hair that usually fell across his eyes was neatly brushed back.

"Peter," she asked, "what's going on?"

Peter shrugged. "Don't know. Jake called and invited us here tonight." He gazed around at the hall. Byte guessed that the evening was just another mystery to him, and he was looking for a clue to solve it.

So much for thinking this was a date, thought Byte.

Mattie and his grandparents, who were struggling to keep up with him, appeared from the other side of the lobby.

"Grandpa got his job back at the museum," Mattie announced. "We're celebrating."

"Yes, I did," Mr. Ramiro said, squeezing Mattie's shoulder and looking at Byte, Peter, and Mr. Braddock. "And I have you all to thank for it. I'm not very good with words, but I want you to know that I—*we*—are very grateful to you."

"Hey, Peter," asked Mattie, "have you heard anything more about the case?"

Peter nodded and looked at his father. The performance hall, with its velvet curtains and marble floors, was a place of quiet and gentle whispers, hardly a place for discussing theft and shootings and the kidnapping of teen detectives. The events of the previous week had taken on a strangely distant quality, as though they had happened years ago or perhaps not at all.

"Well—yes," Peter said. "It looks as if Roarke and Krohg are all but convicted. Finnerman has promised to testify against both of them."

"He's lost his job with InterTel," added Mr. Braddock, "but the police are dropping the charges against him in exchange for his full cooperation."

Finnerman's confession that he stole the chip for Roarke and set up the hologram projector had led to the indictments of both Roarke and Krohg. The 1286dx was locked in an FBI evidence room, and soon it would be returned to InterTel.

The six of them took their seats in the performance hall. They sat in the second row.

Several minutes later a group of men and women strode out onto the stage. The women were wearing formal black dresses, and the men were wearing black tuxedos. All were carrying instruments. They filed onto the stage silently, but one of the tuxedo-clad men slipped out of the line and headed toward Byte and her friends. He was tall—and attractive, Byte thought—and it was a full five seconds before anyone in the group recognized that it was Jake.

"Whoa, check you out," exclaimed Mattie.

Jake offered a weak smile, and he looked, Byte thought, more than a little pale. Mostly, though, he looked happy as he fidgeted with a clarinet.

"Jake," said Byte, "are you?..."

He let out a short laugh. "Um, yeah. I didn't want to tell you guys before in case I didn't make the grade.

I'm going to be playing clarinet tonight with the city jazz band."

The others looked at each other, silent in their amazement.

"I have to go," said Jake, "but I wanted to tell you something real quick. I have something for you." He dug his hand into his tuxedo jacket and fished out a thick stack of small white cards. They looked like business cards. Jake handed some to each of his friends. "My dad quit his job with the printing company and got a small business loan. He's opening up his own printing shop—you know, signs, banners, business cards, that sort of thing. This was his first project." Jake was glowing. "Me and Mom are real proud of him."

Peter looked at one of the cards, and his face broke into a broad grin.

Onstage the conductor frowned and waved at Jake. The musicians had almost finished readying themselves, and he wanted Jake to get back into place.

"Oops, gotta go," said Jake. He hurried to his seat.

Peter sat next to Byte. He smiled at her a little strangely, but she didn't know what it meant. Her gaze locked on the performers.

A few moments passed while the musicians tuned their instruments, the hall echoing with the random harmonies of trumpet and trombone, of clarinet and oboe. It was not music—not yet—but Byte found the sound quite pleasant. It was like many bells ringing all at once.

Then the real music started.

The lights over the audience dimmed, the stage lights rose, and the conductor raised his baton. He swept it down in an arc, and the twenty-five musicians began to play. Minutes later, he pointed the baton toward the clarinet section, and the trumpets, trombones, French horns, and tuba went silent. In the silence, a single clarinet began improvising a lengthy solo.

Byte smiled. *That's Jake.* She looked over at Peter.

He was listening to the music, but his mind seemed to be elsewhere. He felt in his jacket pocket and removed one of the business cards Jake had given him. *Misfits, Inc.* It was a good name. Peter kept the card in his hand for the rest of the evening.

Every few minutes Byte watched him steal a glance at it. He stared at the card, and the tiniest shadow of a grin flickered across his face.